PARTNER SWAP

A collection of twenty erotic stories

Edited by Miranda Forbes

Published by Xcite Books Ltd – 2011
ISBN 9781907761744

Copyright © Xcite Books Ltd 2011

The stories contained within this book are works of fiction. Names and characters are the product of the authors' imaginations and any resemblance to actual persons, living or dead, is entirely coincidental.

All rights reserved. No part of this book may be reproduced, stored in a retrieval system, or transmitted in any form or by any means, electronic, electrostatic, magnetic tape, mechanical, photocopying, recording or otherwise, without the written permission of the publishers: Xcite Books, Suite 11769, 2nd Floor, 145-157 St John Street, London EC1V 4PY

Printed and bound by CPI Group (UK) Ltd, Croydon, CR0 4YY

Cover design by
Madamadari

One-Way Swap was first published in *Naked for Mistress* (2010)

Contents

One Item or Fewer	Elizabeth Coldwell	1
Belle de Nuit	Viva Jones	12
Date Night	Mary Borsellino	23
My Old Dress	Gary Philpott	32
Party Favour	Fierce Dolan	44
Tied Up in Knots	Antonia Adams	59
Rockin' It Old School	Lynn Lake	69
Good Neighbours	Angel Propps	80
That Girl!	Landon Dixon	89
Alive	Clarice Clique	102
The Couple with the Dragon Tattoo	Giselle Renarde	116
Intrigued	Sommer Marsden	130
Quay Party	Courtney James	138
Like a Moth to a Flame	Elizabeth Black	149
Kicks	Landon Dixon	162
Forgotten Desires	Tony Haynes	171
One-Way Swap	Alex Jordaine	182
Deeds of Mercy	Giselle Renarde	193
Pattie and Annette	Penelope Friday	203
Coming Home	Dee Jaye	209

One Item or Fewer
by Elizabeth Coldwell

The dress hangs in front of the wardrobe, whisper thin. You watched me hold it up to my body earlier, imagining how it would look when I put it on. 'You'll be able to see everything,' you said, but the lustful tone in your voice made it clear that's not a bad thing. After all, the point of tonight is to be daring in a way I never have before.

I've been looking forward to Rob's party ever since we received the invitation. It's become an annual institution, every Midsummer's Night without fail. Rob is one of those unfortunate people whose birthday falls in the week between Christmas and New Year, so tends to get lost in the wider celebrations. When he was a kid, his parents used to compensate by throwing him a special summer party. It's a tradition he revived as soon as he moved into the house he owns now, with its big, high-ceilinged rooms and sprawling garden.

And this won't be any old party. There's always a theme, a dress code to be followed. There have been some memorable ones over the years: *Vampires And Virgins*, *Roaring Twenties*, *At The Bottom Of The Sea*. Everyone competes to see who can wear the best costume, but it's always been noticeable how many of the women take it as an excuse to wear an outfit that's as revealing as they can possibly get away with. I swear if the theme was *Night Of*

The Living Dead, Rob's house would be crawling with slutty zombies. So this year, now his divorce is final and he's off the leash at last, he's taken their exhibitionistic tendencies to their natural conclusion, by making this a "one garment only" party.

I emerge from the bathroom freshly showered, wrapped in a fluffy bath sheet that conceals far more of me than the dress will tonight. As I smooth body butter into my legs and blow-dry my hair to a tousled bedhead, I keep casting glimpses at the indecent little outfit, wondering if I'll really have the courage to wear it. If I don't, it'll be a waste of an afternoon spent carefully removing the outer lace sheath from the taupe satin interior. With that lining, the dress was pretty but safe. Without it ...

'Taxi'll be here in ten minutes, Honor,' you remind me. It's OK for you. You've been dressed and ready for ages; your one garment a favourite pair of baggy blue beach shorts. They show off your nicely muscular thighs and a belly that's as flat as it was the day we met, ten years ago, but they hardly drag you out of your comfort zone. Still, tonight's about me, not you. We both know that. If everything goes to plan, tonight will be the night you finally share me with another man.

I usher you out of the room so I can finish getting ready in peace. Taking a deep breath, I drop the towel and step into my dress. It zips up with a soft rasp, and I risk a glance at my reflection. As we'd hoped, the loose floral pattern of the lace hides nothing. My nipples are visible, already beginning to pucker with the excitement of seeing myself so scantily clad. So is the fluff of pubic hair I've trimmed down to a triangle so small it may as well not be there at all. If you were here, now, instead of waiting patiently downstairs, I know you'd be tempted to just forget about the party and fuck me where I stand. Not that I'd object, but I need other people to see me like this. I need Rob to see me.

A horn hoots in the street outside. The taxi is early, and I slip on my coat before grabbing my bag. No sneaky preview for you before we get to the party.

If the driver wonders why my coat is buttoned to the neck on such an unseasonably sultry June night, he doesn't say anything. You've thrown on a hooded sweat top, still Mr Casual as we slide into the back seat together. Your hand is itching to slide up beneath the coat, to take advantage of my knickerless state, but I thwart you by linking my fingers with yours.

'Not yet, darling,' I whisper tenderly in your ear as the taxi pulls away from the kerb. 'It'll be worth the wait, trust me.'

There's hardly any traffic parked on the quiet lane where Rob lives. I can't work out if that means we're among the first to arrive or if, like us, the other guests are choosing to take taxis so they can enjoy a couple of glasses of Rob's deliciously potent punch without the fear of being over the limit.

Rob greets us at the door, beaming broadly. He's dressed more conservatively than I'd expected, in a pair of shorts that are no shorter and no tighter than yours, but he looks good. Positively edible, in fact. The sun has bleached white-blond spikes in his fair hair, and his lean, compact body is lightly tanned. His garden is so secluded, so perfect for sunbathing naked, I can't help wondering whether there is white flesh beneath those shorts or if every last inch of him is that same enticing shade of honey.

'Owen, Honor, great to see you.' He accepts the bottle of Australian Shiraz you hand him with a nod of appreciation. 'You can leave your coats and shoes in the closet by the downstairs loo, then come through to the garden. I'm serving drinks out there.'

When I shrug the coat off my shoulders, your mouth gapes open like a landed fish. Your eyes seem to burn into my hardly concealed tits. Those shorts of yours give little away, but I'm sure you're stiffening inside them.

Grabbing me in a hug that tells me everything I need to know about the state of your cock, you murmur, 'You look fucking amazing.'

'Do you think Rob's going to like it?' I ask.

'Honor, he looks at you like he wants to jump your bones when you're in a sweater and jeans. Dressed like that ...' You don't need to say any more. The feel of your hard-on is giving me all the reassurance I need.

Walking out into the garden, we're greeted with the sight of a dozen or so of Rob's friends and colleagues, as close to naked as we have ever seen them. A couple of the guys have had fun with the dress code. One of Rob's football-playing mates has come in a wetsuit. Another is in a pale pink all-in-one that, coupled with his shaven head, has the effect of making him look like an oversized baby.

Everyone else seems to be taking it more seriously, though I'm not quite sure what category the man in the Borat-style lime green mankini falls into. The strips of Lycra that comprise his costume reveal a surprisingly hairy body, with thick black tufts sprouting on his chest, back and shoulders. There's even a darkish, peachy fuzz on his admittedly spectacular arse. I have to admire his confidence in carrying off such an unbelievably skimpy costume, but my fantasies have never leaned towards men who come complete with their own fur coat.

Several of the women are in lingerie, mostly pretty

teddies and full-length slips, though one girl from Rob's old office, who's always loved showing off her body whatever the theme might be, wears only a pair of ruffled pink stripper knickers. The ties on the side beg to be undone, and I'm sure that once the booze really starts to flow, she'll end up as naked as she's no doubt hoping.

Another couple, who always make a point of coordinating what they wear, are in plain black T-shirts, which finish only an inch or so below crotch level. What, in other circumstances, would be one of the most boring things you can wear is completely subverted by the fact they're both bare beneath those T-shirts. One careless movement and her pussy, his cock, will be exposed to anyone who might be looking. And I'm looking, particularly as his T-shirt appears to be tented slightly at the front by the beginnings of a healthy erection.

While I'm being distracted by all the flesh so blatantly on display, you're striding towards the table where Rob has set out the drinks. A woman I recognise as Rob's former boss, a no-nonsense Yorkshire lass made good, raises her drink in greeting as I follow behind you. Her outfit of choice is a stunning silver mink coat – fake, I assume, though I don't doubt she could afford the real thing if she chose.

She catches me eyeing her. 'Well, people are always saying I'm all fur coat and no knickers, so I thought I'd prove it.'

'Bet you wish you'd worn something a little cooler,' you say.

Her laugh is forged from pure nicotine. 'Don't worry, love. If I get too hot, this is coming right off.'

That's when I realise this party is a couple of glasses of punch away from becoming a full-blown orgy. The girl in the stripper knickers has a pierced nipple, I can't help but notice, the silver barbell that adorns it glittering in the evening sun. Normally, I wouldn't consider another woman in a sexual way, but my mind drifts to what it might be like to take that nipple in my mouth, feeling the barbell cold against my tongue...

'Penny for them,' a voice says, as a glass of something red and fruity, topped with a paper umbrella, is pressed into my hand. I take a sip, tasting rum and plenty of it.

'Oh, I was just taking in the view,' I reply, turning to face Rob. 'You've outdone yourself with this punch, by the way.'

'Oh, it's just a little something of my own invention. I call it Wild And Willing.'

'Which pretty much sums up everyone here.' I'm aware of you, watching me from two feet away, silently giving me your permission to be as flirty with Rob as I want.

'Yeah, they've really embraced the theme of the party. As, I'm pleased to see, have you.' His tone grows lower, more conspiratorial. 'Your tits look fantastic in that dress.'

The words have my cunt twitching with lust, and if I pushed my fingers between my legs I know they'd come away wet. I've wanted Rob for so long, and tonight you're going to let me have him. I feel light headed and giddy, and it has nothing to do with the punch.

Behind us, there's a sudden squeal, answered by a burst of laughter. It alerts us to the fact the girl with the pierced nipple is no longer wearing her elaborate knickers. A bloke in tiny yellow Speedos that leave nothing to the imagination is waving them above his head, while the Borat-alike and a couple of his friends cheer him on. She's making a half-hearted attempt to grab them back, but it's obvious she's loving the fact everyone can now see her cleanly shaved pussy.

'Good job you've got no neighbours,' you comment to Rob. 'Can I top up your punch, Honor?'

I look at my glass, realise I've almost drained it without noticing. You take it from me, giving me the excuse to be alone with Rob just a moment longer. It feels like we're standing in the still eye of a hurricane, while the madness rages around us. Even so, I want to be somewhere else. Somewhere private, where I can act on the ever-deepening need I have to see Rob stripped of those baggy shorts.

You must be reading my mind, because when you return with our drinks, you utter the words that are guaranteed to raise the stakes. 'Rob, you know I wouldn't mind if you fucked Honor.'

Rob's face is a picture as he tries to work out if he's heard you correctly.

You pull me to you with your free hand, stroking my nipple with your thumb almost absent-mindedly. 'She's all yours if you want her. All I ask is that I'm there to join in.'

'Are you OK with this?' Rob asks me, as though alarmed by my silence on the matter.

Truth is, I haven't been able to say anything, because I'm so churned up with giddy anticipation. Inside, though, I'm screaming at you to say yes. Somehow I manage to find my voice.

'I want this. We want this. What do you say, Rob?'

'Well, I shouldn't really leave my guests unattended ...' As we glance round, we see that Mr Speedos is now kissing the girl he stripped of her knickers, his hands kneading the cheeks of her arse as she grinds herself on to his swimwear-clad bulge.

'I think they can manage without us,' you comment, in

a tone as dry as the Sahara.

'Let's go inside,' Rob says. As we walk up the path towards the house, you holding one of my hands, Rob holding the other, no one pays us the slightest attention. Perhaps our disappearance will be their cue to unleash the pent-up lust that hovers just beneath the surface of this gathering, pair off and fuck on the lawn.

I've been in Rob's house so many times, but I don't think I've ever seen the inside of his bedroom. It's a single man's room, all right; the bed's king-sized but the duvet is rumpled, the pillows scattered everywhere. There's a portable TV with a built-in DVD player on top of the chest of drawers, angled so he'll be able to watch it in bed. Prominently on the top of the pile of DVDs beside it is a box featuring a busty model dressed as a schoolgirl and licking a lollipop, her nipples hard and prominent through the shirt knotted beneath her midriff. A vision flashes into my mind: Rob, propped up against the pillows, slowly stroking his cock as, on screen, the girl in the porno has her tight white knickers pulled down and her arse soundly spanked.

Rob spots what I'm looking at, and flashes me an unrepentant grin. The vision changes, and now it's my arse he's spanking. The thought gets me hot and bothered all over again, but I'm still not sure how we're going to kick this little threesome off.

That's when you take control. 'Go on, Rob. Strip her.'

Given that I'm almost naked as it is, all Rob has to do is tug down the zip. The grating as the teeth are pulled apart seems crazily loud and I realise we're all holding our breath, aware of the growing tension in the room. I step out of the skimpy lace sheath. Rob pulls me into his arms and we kiss. His mouth tastes of rum punch and his lips are surprisingly soft.

We collapse on to the bed, mouths still mashed together. At your urging, I free his cock from his shorts, and stroke the fat, veined length of it. Somehow your hand works its way between my legs, finding my slick pussy. You're determined not to be a passive spectator. Instead, you're directing us to move into a position that gives you easier access to my clit. Happy to oblige, I kneel up, giving you a perfect view of my sex lips as they pout at you. Your finger traces teasingly along them, and I almost lose my grip on Rob's cock

'Nice and juicy,' you murmur. 'Perfect for fucking.'

I know you want to watch Rob screw me first, and by now I'm more than ready to have that gorgeous tool inside me.

You fish for something in the pocket of your shorts, tossing it to Rob. 'Time to rubber up, mate.'

He rolls the condom down on to his erection. Considerate as ever, you've made sure the latex is ribbed – for my pleasure. Not that you're not loving what's happening too. Though I can't even begin to know what's going on inside your head, at the moment where your most cherished fantasy is finally about to be brought to panting, sweating life.

Poising myself over Rob's groin, I guide his cock into place and sink down. So used to your dimensions, it takes me a moment to adjust to his extra girth. Catching sight of myself in his mirrored wardrobe door, I almost laugh at the wide-eyed surprise on my face.

As I feel him sliding slowly into me, I look over at you. Your shorts are off and you're stroking yourself deliberately. You give me a wide smile of love and gratitude, and I can't help returning it. How many years has it been since I've had sex with anyone other than you? It certainly hasn't grown boring in all that time, but now the strangeness is wearing off, I'm relishing having another man inside me.

Sounds drift in through the open window, laughter and what could be a man's deep grunting, and I wonder what's happening down in the garden. It's only a brief distraction. Rob is reaching up to grab my tits, pinching my nipples roughly. Fired up by his caresses, I grind down hard, matching his ferocity with my own. With a despairing groan, Rob's body stiffens beneath me, and he hangs on to my hips, keeping me still as he comes.

He pulls out, flopping on his side on the bed as you take his place. You urge me up on my hands and knees, wanting to take me from behind. Easing your way into my depths, you hold steady for a moment. Your voice is an excited growl in my ear. 'I can tell he's stretched you just a little. Did it feel good?'

'It felt absolutely brilliant,' I reply sincerely. 'But so do you.'

It's no word of a lie. Without the impediment of a condom – the privilege all those years of monogamy affords you – your cock is hot and vital inside me. You thrust into me with hard, fast strokes. Rob reaches over and toys with my hanging breasts, then turns his attention to my clit, rolling it between his fingers.

You make a strange, strangled noise in your throat, and when I check our reflection, I realise that as Rob is playing with me, the heel of his palm keeps catching your balls. The movement can't be anything but deliberate, and from the look on your face it's not unpleasant, either. Seems I hadn't considered all the possibilities when two men and a woman start to have fun together. Maybe I should start giving them some serious thought.

But thinking seriously about anything is getting harder, given the combination of Rob's finger work and your remorselessly thrusting cock. Seems like having you work on me in tandem has wound every nerve, every fibre in my body as taut as it has ever been. Just when I think I can't take a moment more of this delicious torment, you shift the pace of your stroking up a gear. That's all it takes for the pleasure coursing through me to reach critical mass. My pussy muscles clench round your shaft as I come harder than I think I ever have, wringing your orgasm from you in the process. Face contorted in ecstasy, the cords in your neck standing out, your bullish roar is so loud they must be able to hear it out in the garden. Not that I care. Slumping into a tangled pile of limbs with you and Rob, everything that matters at this moment is right here.

'So how was it?' you ask eventually.

'Wonderful,' I reply, taking the time to kiss each of you in turn. There's so much more I want to add. How this evening has surpassed anything I could have dreamed of. How I wish we'd had the courage to try this ages ago, and how much I want to try sucking your cock while Rob fucks me. Or – and this thought really intrigues me – watch him suck your cock, instructing him to take you deep into his throat. Instead, forcing myself to think about what might be happening down on the lawn, I ask, 'Don't we have a party to get back to?'

In synchrony, the two of you shake your heads. Then Rob, making it perfectly clear where he'd rather be, slithers down my body to lick the last oozing remnants of your come from my pussy, and our own private party begins all over again, with not even one garment to impede our fun.

Belle de Nuit
by Viva Jones

The hotel bar had slick beige and chocolate-coloured panelled walls, soft, sensuous lighting and chairs the colour of Caribbean sand. Kara sat at the bar, sipping a vodka martini. She was a natural beauty, with black, shoulder-length hair that framed her finely-boned face. Her dark eyes were emphasised with smoky-grey eye shadow and her lips were the shade of rich burgundy, to match her nails. She was wearing a tight-fitting asymmetrical black dress, and it showed off her slender figure and the taut breasts which really didn't need a bra. Her legs, as toned as a young colt's, were lengthened even more by a pair of strappy gun-heeled shoes.

She looked edgy but rich, sensual but intriguing.

A man in his late 30s approached her – he had dark hair and eyes and was wearing a navy blazer over a pair of pale chinos. He was handsome enough and looked wealthy. She caught the barman's eye, but almost imperceptibly, he shook his head.

'I'm waiting for someone,' she told the disappointed stranger, indicating the stool beside her own. 'This seat's taken.'

She waited a few more minutes, sipping her martini, until another man entered, looking around until his eyes settled on her. He was wearing an elegantly-cut suit and had thick, dark hair that contained greying flecks she'd always found attractive. Without hesitating, he approached her as if he'd known her all his life – it was the kind of self-assurance she'd always looked for, and usually found, in a lover.

Kara checked the barman, and this time he gave her a discreet nod.

'Is anyone sitting here?' He indicated the stool next to hers.

'Only the invisible man.'

He sat down. 'A Jack Daniels, please,' he asked the barman, who gave Kara a complicit smile. 'My name's Brad.' He held his hand out.

'Kara,' she responded, shaking his hand. 'And I'll have a vodka martini.'

He ordered her drink. 'Asides the invisible man, were you waiting for someone, Kara?'

'Only if the right person showed up.'

He smiled, trying to understand her. Why would a beautiful woman, dressed to kill like that, be sitting alone in a hotel bar? 'You live in the neighbourhood?'

'I have a suite here, at the hotel. It suits my purposes.'

'Is that right? And what purposes may they be?'

Kara just smiled mysteriously and toyed with her glass. 'And what's a nice American boy doing in a dirty European city like this?' she asked him.

'I'm handling a corporate takeover. A chain of deluxe European hotels, discreet and stylish. This is one of them, as a matter of fact.'

'It'd be a good buy.'

'Too right. I'm having trouble with the major shareholder, though. Guy's like, half-dead from a stroke, but he's still playing hard ball. Claims he won't sell at any price. Hell, we all know that everything's got a price.'

'Everything? Is that so, now?' Kara shrugged, as if no longer interested in the conversation. 'Did you do your due diligence on the rooms?'

He looked at her, surprised, but then he smiled, and his smile was boyish but electrically charged: it was the kind of smile that could make a girl forget her own name. 'There's a suite I've yet to see.'

Kara paused and nodded towards the gold band on his finger. 'Nice ring you've got there.'

The smile turned to embarrassment. 'Twelve years, three kids,' he admitted. 'Not to mention a business dinner in a little over an hour. Too bad. We could have had some fun.'

'Yes, too bad.' Kara agreed with a resigned smile. 'We could have had a lot of fun.'

Brad had just ordered two more drinks when his mobile rang. 'Hello? Oh, I'm sorry to hear that, sir … I hope you feel better in the morning … I understand, of course. Take good care of yourself, now.'

'Problem?'

'The stroke guy. Had some kind of attack, only a minor one, but enough to cancel on me.' He sighed theatrically. 'So tell me? What do you suggest a man should do alone tonight in a city like this?'

'I can think of a thing or two.'

'That suite you mentioned earlier …?'

'Same colour scheme as this, but with a mirror, strategically positioned opposite the bed.'

Kara stared into Brad's chocolate-coloured eyes, willing him to take a chance.

'Listen, I er …' Brad struggled to find the right words. 'Forgive me if I'm misreading the situation or something. Can I just be forward and lay down some ground rules here? I'm a happily married man, as you already noticed, but I've been three weeks on the road, and that's an awful long time. You're an extraordinarily attractive and desirable woman, and I'd have to be as half-dead as that stubborn shareholder of ours not to want you.'

Kara considered this for a moment. 'Are you propositioning me?'

'I guess I am. I totally did not expect to be unfaithful to my wife during this trip, but I'm tired and I'm pissed that negotiations aren't going my way and I need a release. Maybe I can make my proposition, as you put it, more attractive? A suite, how much has that got to cost? Five hundred, would that cover it?'

She paused to consider. 'You'd use a condom, and there'd be nothing weird.'

'I agree to those terms.'

'Cash.'

'You got it.'

They rode the lift up to the top floor, careful to appear like two strangers, oblivious of each other's presence, and she led him quickly down the corridor to her suite. Its living room was chic and impersonal and smelt of the oversized pink lilies that perched on a glass coffee table in the centre. Taking Brad's hand, Kara led him through to the bedroom, where a king-sized bed awaited them. On the opposite wall was an equally king-sized mirror.

'Do you like to watch?' Kara asked.

'I never have before,' he told her. 'But there's a first time for everything.'

He pulled her close and kissed her, deeply and urgently. Then he unzipped her dress and let it fall to the ground. Underneath, she was wearing a black, lacy bra, French-style knickers and a pair of stockings and suspenders. As he admired her body, he pulled off his tie and unbuttoned his shirt, while she began tugging at his belt. As his trousers hit the ground his cock was already springing out of his boxer shorts, and Kara was pleased to see that it was hard, and of above-average size.

She pulled him towards the edge of the bed, so they were in full view of the mirror. Then, she took his cock in her mouth and licked it, studying her own reflection. Next, she opened her mouth wider and swallowed it as deep as she could.

'Oh Jesus, that feels good,' he sighed, losing himself in the sensation. 'Not too much, though, it's been three weeks already, remember?' He pulled her up and, through her bra, stroked her breasts, teasing the fabric away from her hardening nipples. 'I don't want to come yet. Not before I've had you every which way I can.'

Kara undid the fastening and let her bra fall to the ground, and he massaged each nipple, dropping down to suck and gently bite them.

'Five hundred buys me whatever I want, right? So keep the stockings and shoes on,' he whispered urgently, twisting her around so she was facing the mirror, and then pushing her gently onto the bed, so her pussy was on the edge. 'Let me just explore what you've got down here first.'

He dropped to the floor, his hands running over her breasts, stomach and the line of Kara's suspenders. Then, making sure she was in full view of the reflection, he ran his fingers across the material of her knickers, before pulling the crotch to one side to expose her pussy.

'Man, that's a beautiful look,' he whispered, turning to admire the view in the mirror. Then he moved his face closer, breathing in her scent, before poking out his tongue and tracing the line of her folds, expertly finding her clit.

'Oh God, that feels good,' she cried out, arching her

back as he carried on teasing her, flicking his tongue as far as the constriction of her knickers would let him.

'Open your legs wider, that's right,' he instructed. 'Man, that's one beautiful pussy you've got.' He inserted two fingers inside her and turned to watch in the mirror as he manoeuvred them in and out. 'I can't wait to fuck you hard.'

Kara's knickers felt wet and uncomfortable, and she longed to take them off. She sat up. 'Come here,' she said assertively. 'We don't want your cock to feel left out.' She pulled him up and, with his boxers still on, took his cock in her mouth again, and she watched herself licking and sucking him, holding the base in one hand and teasing his balls with the other.

'You're so big,' she gasped. 'I don't know if I can take you.'

'We'll get you nice and wet first.'

She pulled back and lowered his boxers to the floor. He had a good, tanned physique, and clearly spent a lot of time at the gym. He sat on the edge of the bed as she took control.

'My panties are all wet,' she told him. 'I've got to take them off.'

He went to help her but she pushed him back, then turned around so that her back was facing the mirror, and in one sweeping movement, her legs straight and body bent forward, she pulled her knickers to the ground until her hands were touching the floor, and she was exposing herself to him in the reflection. Then she stepped out of them and kicked them to one side, opening her legs wider. He gasped as he admired her firm buttocks and the secrets they could no longer conceal – the dark pink of her anus, the gaping readiness of her pussy, the glistening wet folds of her cunt.

Turning her around, so they were now sideways on, he held her by her hips and placed his face close to her, and began to slide his tongue up and down and in and out until she was nearly screaming with pleasure, watching him doing so in the mirror.

'I want you inside me now,' she urged. 'I'm going to come any minute, but I want to feel your enormous great cock inside me first!'

As Brad produced a condom from his inner jacket pocket, she dived between his legs and took his cock in her mouth again. After taking him as deep as she could, she pulled back and watched as he put the condom on.

Next, she pushed him down so he was sitting on the edge of the bed, and then climbed on top of him, opening her buttocks and pussy lips with her fingers so he could get a good view in the mirror. She slid her wet pussy over his cock a couple of times, sighing as it stroked her clit, before pushing herself down on him, luxuriating in his size and how he filled her. After a few minutes of her thrusting on top of him, Brad took charge again, flipping her over and lowering her on to the bed, opening her legs wide. Then he stopped to look at her reflection in the mirror, and not satisfied with what he saw, swung her around so that they were sideways on, before climbing on top and sliding his cock inside her.

Holding her knees down to steady himself, he slid in and out, slowly and deliberately, filling her and emptying her, until the pace of her breathing quickened.

'You can't come yet,' he whispered. 'I'm not done with you yet. I want to see every position, from every angle. You up for the challenge?'

Kara could only moan in response. Brad pulled out and flipped her on to her stomach. Then he pulled up her bottom and, pausing to study her reflection, climbed on top and slid inside her again. He was thrusting harder now, and she gasped with his every thrust. Then he pulled out as abruptly as he'd slid in, and flipped them both over, so he was now lying on his back, and she was on top of him, and they were full on once again in the mirror.

'I love to see your ass in the reflection,' he whispered, holding her buttocks. 'It totally fucking turns me on.'

His eyes on the mirror, he started gently stroking her anus, before easing his middle finger inside. She gasped and pushed back, welcoming it deeper and deeper.

For the third time she was about to come when he changed position. This time, he pulled her up so she was virtually standing, her back to the mirror, with her arms supporting her on the edge of the bed. Holding her tight, he entered her from behind, spreading her legs wide, and then started sliding his middle finger around her clit, stroking her while holding her firmly down on his cock.

'Let me come, you bastard,' she screamed out, fearing that if she didn't come soon, she'd lose it altogether. 'Let me come!'

'One last thing.'

Now, Brad manoeuvred himself on to the bed in full view of the mirror, and pulled her on top of him, also on her back. Her legs wide open and pussy completely exposed to the mirror, he slid his cock inside her again and, while slowly thrusting, kept stroking her pussy, alternately running his middle and index fingers up and down her folds, and circling her clit.

'Oh Jesus, this time you've got to let me come,' she begged him. 'If I don't I'll go crazy.'

Suddenly Kara exploded in a rush of hedonistic, voyeuristic pleasure, coming in gasps and screams, thrusting harder and harder for what felt like hours. When her orgasm finally subsided, Brad came too, gasping and grunting, pushing himself inside her until she thought she might split open.

She stayed limply on top of him for a few minutes until his cock started its inevitable slide out of her. Then she rolled off and they lay, spent, beside each other, drenched in each other's sweat. In the end, it was Brad who broke the silence.

'That has to go down as the most amazing fuck of my life,' he said. 'You have a magnificent cunt. And ass. And tits. And everything that goes with them. That's a fuck I'm going to remember for the rest of my life.'

'Yes, I think it is,' Kara agreed, without emotion. 'You know, the Chinese believe that a mirror in the bedroom brings bad luck,' she went on. 'If your soul wakes up in the night and sees its own reflection, it gets startled and creates nightmares.'

'Is that so?' he asked in a gently mocking tone. 'In that case, let's be thankful we're not Chinese,' he added, getting up and heading for the bathroom. 'Because I, for one, wholeheartedly approve. I don't see myself having nightmares over this any time soon.'

As Kara heard the shower start, she smiled at the mirror. 'Don't you, now?'

She sat up, staring thoughtfully at her own reflection, while he showered. She pulled one leg up so that her knee supported her chin, and her pussy was once again exposed. She could still smell sex on her body, and she liked it. When Brad emerged, clean and wholesome and reeking of expensive shower gel, he dressed quickly, before pulling out some notes from his wallet and handing them over. Wordlessly, she put them in her handbag.

He looked at her, not understanding who she was, or where she belonged. 'Are you with an agency or something?'

'I like to work independently.'

'Do you have a card? You know, for when I'm in town again?'

'No, I don't,' she told him bluntly. 'Consider that a one-off.'

He was embarrassed, now that he was clean and dressed and ready to leave, to see her nakedness, and to smell the scent of their sex still on her skin. He hadn't intended to be unfaithful to his wife, Kara could see that, and the regrets were beginning to mount. 'Well, thank you,' he told her awkwardly. 'Like I said, that was the most unforgettable fuck of my life.'

'You're welcome,' she said with a smile. 'And you have a good trip home.'

'Not before I finish this deal,' he told her, his awkwardness turning to arrogance. 'That sucker's got to sell, and on my terms.' He'd reached the door. 'Wow,' he cried out with an incredulous laugh. 'What an unbelievable fuck!'

Once the door had slammed behind him, Kara got up, and, still wearing nothing but her stockings, suspenders and strappy shoes, approached the mirror, searching down one side for a release. Instantly, the mirror swung open, revealing a small room full of recording equipment, in which sat an elderly man in a wheelchair.

'Hope you enjoyed the show?'

'Congratulations, my dear,' the old man told her. 'You excelled yourself tonight.'

He pulled her towards him and tenderly kissed her small strip of pubic hair, breathing in her scent. Then, he put his hand in his pocket and pulled out a wedding ring, which he passed to her. Kara slipped it on her finger.

'I get little pleasure these days,' he went on. 'But that was outstanding. I might not be able to satisfy your physical needs myself any more, but it's a joy to watch someone else do so. And he seemed particularly capable in that department.'

'He was. Outstanding. Did you get the pictures?'

'More than enough. If those bastards think they can buy me out, they've got another thing coming. I refuse to hand my life's work over to some tawdry American chain. At breakfast he'll be hand-delivered an envelope containing the best images, and the accompanying note will make it clear that both his wife and chairman shall receive the same unless he backs away from this deal. You did a fine job.'

Kara kissed the top of her husband's head. Before his stroke he'd been a dynamic, ruthless businessman who'd built up an international portfolio of high-end hotels and retail outlets. She'd worked as his legal consultant, and their ensuing affair had resulted in marriage. Despite his obsession with business, he'd been a compassionate and loving partner. He might only be a shell of that man today, but Kara still cared about him. In return, he had no doubts as to his wife's abilities. She'd inherit his legacy, and as major shareholder, would take control of all operations.

As he replayed the moment of her orgasm on the television monitor, Kara took a certain pride in his pleasure. Some might have found it perverted, but to her their Saturday night amusements had become the most natural thing in the world. There had been plenty of lovers, and plenty of shows in front of the reflective glass, but none had been as important as this.

When Kara stopped to think about it, there was little she couldn't bring herself to do for her husband, or for her future.

Date Night
by Mary Borsellino

Her name was Amanda – not Amy, not Mandy, always Amanda – and I wanted to watch Frank fuck her from the first moment I met her.

She was the new girl at my office, working in the accounts department, and she was exactly the sort of girl Frank liked (when he didn't like girls like me, that is). Amanda was petite and fine-boned, with a peaches-and-cream complexion and strawberry blonde hair which curled around her sharp little face and long, slim neck.

She laughed often and had a crooked, slightly sardonic smile, and drank her coffee black with sugar. I liked her instantly and completely, and told Frank about her as soon as I got home from work that day.

I'm a little taller than Amanda and a lot less thin. Not in a miserable self-loathing way, of course – my curves are lush and beautiful, and Frank adores them. I have dark brown hair, long but kept tied back from my face usually. My eyes are a light hazel. Frank's are as well, so I suppose if we have children some day they'll be bound to inherit that trait. The rest of the mix between our genes will be less predictable.

Frank is tall and broad, and makes me feel tiny beside him. He has a neatly trimmed beard of a sandier, more golden blond than Amanda's hair. His own hair is the same shade as his beard, shot through with the first strands of silvery grey. He's older than me by 15 years, and I'm 35. He doesn't look 50, but there's a distinguished wisdom in his expressions sometimes which makes me feel like the naughty young student who has somehow managed to seduce the professor.

Amanda wasn't the first woman I'd wanted to watch my husband bed, by any means, but she was one of the most exciting to pursue. I began to find out little pieces of information about her, like a spy learning the background Intel on a mark.

'Mark and I got married last September,' she told me one morning when we were catching a few moments of fresh air during our break. 'We wanted to wait until he finished his degree. I was such a wild girl before him – I know it's hard to believe that, now.'

Amanda chuckled self-consciously, tucking some hair behind her ear and ducking her head away from my gaze. As if she was worried I'd laugh at her or something. But she wasn't anywhere near as boring and sedate as she seemed to think she was. There was a subtle sensuality to her movements, a richness in her laugh, that spoke volumes about secret facets of her personality.

'In fact,' she went on. 'I've joked with him sometimes that I stole his innocence. He's only two years younger than me, really, but I was his first girlfriend. I couldn't believe it when he told me that; how could someone as beautiful as him be ignored?'

I'd seen the photo of Mark she kept in her wallet. Like Amanda, he had an unassuming, mild sort of face, the kind that is more pleasant than compelling. I understood how he could have been ignored by the girls of his school and university; the charms of a man like him were only visible to an eye like Amanda's, just as her beauty was apparent to me but hidden from most.

'He didn't steal your innocence in return?' I asked, already having a fair guess as to what her answer would be.

Another throaty chuckle. 'Not exactly.'

I could have made a move then, an arch overture hinting at the delights which Frank and I could offer the younger couple, but I left things as they were and filed the newly discovered information away for later use.

Frank heard all about the conversation that evening, my words broken by stutters and gasps for air as he bent me over the arm of one of our soft leather couches and entered me from behind. My crisp pinstripe skirt was shoved up to my hips, the fabric bunching up in unrefined wrinkles as his broad hands held me exactly where he wanted me. My tights were a tangle at my ankles, along with my black satin panties, and I was so wet and ready that I felt as if all the blood in my body was flushing the plump lips of my labia, making them fat and slick and purple.

I moaned, I bit back screams, I came and came. And between the unrelenting, almost cruelly wonderful waves of ecstasy, I told Frank about Amanda and about Mark.

'She told me they have a weekly date night. They go to a film and then a late dinner,' I managed to grunt out, the short nail of his thumb flicking back and forth over my clit as he fucked me hard.

'Date night? Kinky?' Frank joked, his own voice breaking a little as another orgasm made me clench down hard around his cock.

'I think we should gatecrash them,' I decided. 'Sound like a plan?'

'An excellent plan,' Frank agreed. After that, we gave up on talking, and let our baser instincts take control.

***

And so we did as we'd planned, and invited ourselves along to Amanda and Mark's date night. It was easy enough to show up at the same movie theatre I knew they went to, and to feign surprise at running into them. There was a suspicious cast to Amanda's eyes as she looked at us, but that didn't deter me: the charade had always been largely for Mark's sake, because I thought it was fairly likely that Frank and I could have had Amanda in our bed without any pretence at all. It was her husband who required seducing.

I sat beside him in the darkened theatre, let my leg brush against his with each of my movements, let myself arch and stretch in just the right way to make my chest thrust forward. My nipples were hard, pressing against the silk lining of my dress, and I let myself make a small purr of pleasure at the chill of the air conditioning against them. I wasn't wearing a bra, and the sensation was making it harder and harder to concentrate on the plot of the film.

After the credits rolled, I stretched my arms above my head and said, 'I think I need a cigarette. Anyone want to come with me?'

As I suspected she would, Amanda just gave me a small, crooked grin and shook her head. 'I'm good. How about Frank and I wait here, and you two go?'

So Mark and I headed out for the roof-top parking lot, underneath a scatter of stars and right in the path of the wind.

'Amanda's told me about you,' Mark said as we lit our cigarettes and inhaled happily. 'And your husband, though she hasn't met him before tonight.'

'All good things, I hope,' I joked gently. It was like trying to catch a skittish rabbit. If I came on too strong,

I'd frighten him off completely.

'She says she thinks you might be swingers,' he replied, and there was something in his voice that told me the unspoken half of his story: these conversations between them had taken place in their bed, after fucking. Or perhaps even during, judging by the excited glimmer in Mark's eyes.

'What do you think?' I asked. 'Think she's right?'

He laughed. He sounded a little nervous, but not so much that he was going to back down.

'I think we're skipping dinner,' he said.

Our bedroom is large and comfortable and furnished in simple, no-nonsense style: it has a big bed, and a closet set into one wall, and an en-suite bathroom, and that's it.

Amanda was clearly more at ease with the situation unfolding than Mark was, so I let her and Frank take the first initiative and move towards the bed, while I pressed Mark up against the solid wood of the now-closed bedroom door and kissed him gently, trying to be as soothing and unthreatening as possible. Finally, after what seemed an age to my already maddened blood, I felt him begin to properly relax, for him to harden against my hip.

I pulled my dress up over my head and started to unbutton his shirt. He did his best to help with the task but his fingers were clumsy, fumbling, so I pushed them away and did the work myself. When he was naked to the waist, I sank to my knees and unzipped his fly, slipping his pants down and off and then following them with his shoes and socks.

He smelled clean and neat, but with an edge of something sharper – this was the sort of boy that a girl like Amanda fell in love with, after all. There were secret complexities to him, secrets in the hitches of his breath and the hectic flush tinting his delicate cheekbones.

'Amanda said she was your first girlfriend,' I remarked, looking up at him from my position in front of him, letting my hands roam restlessly over the sparse dark hair on his pale thighs. The front of his navy blue boxer-briefs was tented, straining where his cock pushed out.

Mark was trembling, ever so slightly. I thought it was probably from the effort of holding himself still, of not arching into my touch. His restraint was charming and infuriating all at once.

I've never been one for restraint myself, and that moment was no exception. My mouth was already watering from greedy lust. 'Mark?' I prompted, letting one of my hands slide up over the fabric of his underwear. Over the leg, as far from his aroused penis as I could force myself to be (I wanted him so much my self-control was shaky at best), up to the elastic waistband. I began easing it down slowly, over skin that shivered with desire at my touch.

'Yes,' he choked out. 'Amanda was my first.'

'Kind of like learning to drive on a Ferrari,' I smirked. 'You must be something special to get a girl like that.'

I rubbed my thumb over the now-bared crease of his hip, then followed the same line with my nose. Smelling, rutting. The scent of him was stronger here, less complicated.

Mark was watching Amanda and Frank. They were quite the sight to behold, golden on golden, her compact thighs spread across his broader hips, riding him in graceful rocking thrusts. Her head was thrown back, her breasts straining against the black lace of the bra still covering them, Frank's fingertips pressed against the curve of the small of her back.

I sucked a wet kiss against Mark's thigh, jolting his

attention back to me, reminding him that his wife wasn't the only one who was going to get her brains fucked out tonight.

Mark's knees trembled violently, threatening to buckle. I was charmed and flattered by the involuntary response, even as it made him blush and stammer with apparent shame. I shushed his apologies away and stood, leading him over to the unoccupied side of the bed, where I guided him down to sit on the edge.

I could have had him lie down, next to Frank, and climbed atop him, but now that I'd given myself the thought of sucking Mark's cock I couldn't easily shake the anticipation for it. The fucking could wait for another night. I was determined this would be but the first of many such adventures between the four of us.

I sank down again, the sensation of carpet under my knees enough to send a jolt of want shooting straight down from my belly. It's amazing how powerful sense-memories can be, when we know they're probably the prelude to something wonderful.

A lot of people don't like sucking cock. They'll do it in exchange for a back rub, or because it's their husband's birthday, or for one of a thousand other reasons. But they don't like it.

Not me. I love it. I love the weight in my mouth, the taste, the way my jaw begins to ache after a little while, the slickness of spit on my lips. I love the noises men make when I do it, like the strangled moan Mark gave when I swallowed him down in one movement.

With one hand, I held his thighs steady. I used the other to play with his balls, to stroke the skin just behind. He was gripping the edge of the bedspread, white-knuckled, and so I pulled back and let his cock slip from my lips with a spit-shiny pop, looking up into his dilated eyes.

'You can pull my hair, it's all right,' I assured him, and slid back down. My own sex was throbbing, almost painfully turned on, but I resisted the urge to slip a hand inside my panties, to match the movement of my head stroke for stroke. After I come hard I get lazy and selfish, and I knew that if I came now it would be a hard one. So I held off, letting my desire spiral up and up to dizzying heights as I sucked Mark's cock.

He lost control fast, the sounds and scents of Amanda and Frank's continued screwing making it seem like the whole world around us was sex, heat and want and need. Mark's already shaky grasp on his better nature was no match for an atmosphere like that, and after a few minutes his hands were knotted in my hair, his hips snapping up in uncontrolled little jerks each time I made my throat ripple in a swallow around the head of his cock.

I rocked a little, back and forth on my knees, letting my whole body enjoy the slow throbs of lust which pulsed through me with each heartbeat. I could feel Mark's heartbeat too, faster than my own, in the thick vein on the underside of his cock. I pressed my tongue up against that pulse, as if to taste the crackling electricity of his life force, and that small motion was enough to set off the climax that had been building in him.

He slid off the edge of the bed, pulling me close against him, the sweat on his narrow chest sticking us together as he licked into my mouth, tasting himself. His tongue was a slick rasp against my swollen, sensitised lips, and I moaned into his mouth.

Mark's fingers, thinner and more tentative than Frank's had ever been against my pussy, pressed against the soaked fabric of my underwear, rubbing in an unrelenting rhythm that made my eyes roll back in my head and my teeth bite down hard on the meat of his shoulder. I came hard, my hands clutching at his upper arms, my knees still pressed against the carpet.

We sat there together, a breathless tangle of clammy limbs, for a long moment. Our bonelessness was interrupted by Amanda, who leaned over the edge of the bed and tilted Mark's head back so she could give him a sloppy, awkward-angled kiss. Her hair was a messy halo around her head and she was still half-draped across Frank's reclining form.

'All our date nights should be this good,' she declared happily. 'What do you think, sweetie?'

Mark laughed softly, the love he had for Amanda clear in his eyes as he stared at her. 'I think I tend to agree,' he replied, and helped me to my feet so we could join the others on the bed.

My Old Dress
by Gary Philpott

I had forgotten about my old dress until the night Carol and her new boyfriend came over. She lived in Singapore, but was on her annual trip to see her family. Knowing she could only stomach her mother in small doses, I invited the two of them over to us for dinner.

Carol and I go back a long way, all the way back to our wild days when we used to go out on the pull together. The only thing that seemed to have changed from my point of view was the fact that she had graduated from one-night stands and two-week flings, to relationships which fizzled out after six months or so. Her latest guy was a Kiwi called Rob. And like all Carol's men, he was gorgeous. My hard drive contains sufficient emailed photographs of him to testify to that fact. I often loiter on one in particular. He is on a hotel balcony wearing just a pair of boxers, a pair of boxers that failed to hide his hard-on. My mind often ponders upon what happened after that photo was taken. It has even been known to lure Mr Buzz out of my drawer.

The thing about Carol is that she has the feminine attributes to attract good looking men, and the sex drive to keep them for as long as she wants. They have to be able to take the pace mind.

My own desire to turn men's heads again is what led to

a particularly raunchy Saturday night. My fitness routines and healthier diet had been on the go for two years, and they were certainly paying dividends.

When the evening arrived, things went pretty much as one might expect during the course of the meal. We caught up on each other's news, told a holiday tale or two, and even dared to venture onto the subject of politics. It was only when we moved through to the sitting room that things got interesting.

'I still can't get over how good you look,' exclaimed Carol, as I opened the obligatory pack of chocolate mint wafers.

'It was hard work, but well worth it.'

'And how about you, Nigel, do you think it was worth it?'

'Definitely, I can hardly keep my hands off her.' He laughed and planted a hand on my bum.

As I held out the box, Carol took two. She popped one into her mouth and held the other up in front of Rob's lips. Her hand moved to his groin at exactly the moment he jerked his head forward to snap the chocolate away with his teeth.

'You've not changed,' I remarked.

'How do you mean?'

I dropped my eyes to her left hand.

'Life's too short not to have fun.' She smiled and gave Rob's tackle a little squeeze.

I turned to offer Nigel a chocolate.

'Do you still wear that red slut dress?' asked Carol from behind me.

It took a moment for me to make sense of her question. 'Oh, I know the one you mean. No, I haven't worn it for years.'

Rob suddenly perked up. 'What dress is this?'

'Nigel will tell you.' Carol pointed a finger at him. 'Susie was wearing it the night he first fucked her.'

'Are you suggesting my wife put out on our first date?' laughed Nigel.

'It wasn't a date, she seduced you in a night club, remember?'

'Oh, yes.' He smiled like a man recalling a very successful evening.

'And you seem to be forgetting the fact that we were best mates, so I know what you two did in the loos. Anyway, it was Susie's fuck-me dress, she always wore it when she was desperate to get laid. You were on a sure thing from the moment she wrapped her arms round you.'

'You bitch,' I smiled.

'No offence, Susie, Nigel must realise what you were like back then. After all, he's turned out to be the main beneficiary of your wanton ways.'

'If you want to talk about my past, I might talk about Corfu.'

'Ooh, confession time. Perhaps we should play confessions.'

'Maybe later,' interrupted Rob. 'Have you got any photos of this dress?'

Carol leant forward. 'I bet she's still got the real thing.'

'As it happens, I have.' It had been stuffed into quite a few charity shop bags over the years, but I always pulled it out again. My flirty side could never let it go.

'Well, what are you waiting for?' She pointed to the ceiling. 'Get upstairs and see if it still fits. I bet it does.' Her eyes ran over my body.

'I'm not sure I …'

'Do it girl, make Rob's day.'

The cogs inside my head began to turn. My best friend was asking me to give her man a bit of a show. And what's more, he seemed very keen on the idea. The thought that I was turning him on was turning me on. Nigel's gentle nod encouraged me to indulge my two guests. I took another gulp from my glass and left the room.

Upstairs in the bedroom I pulled the dress out of the awkward to get at end of my wardrobe. The bass of some music penetrated the floorboards from below. I recognised it as the compilation Nigel often put on when he was feeling horny. Within minutes I was naked and excited. I pulled the dress over my head, just as I had done many times in my early 20s. It resisted a little as I pulled it down over my hips, but then it always did. I ran my hands down the sides of my body. It felt so figure hugging, and so smooth. I stepped over to the mirror to see if it looked as good as it felt. I was not disappointed.

It was deep scarlet with a hem that sat halfway up my thighs. The back plunged down to the top of my bum. Two strips of narrow fabric ran over each breast and met inches above my navel. They were held together with criss-crossing straps that started under my bust. I turned sideways to check out the teasing side view of my tits that had turned so many men to jelly in the past. My hardened nipples only added to the sexiness of it all.

The shoes I always wore with the dress had been thrown out long ago. The only red heels I have in my collection now are the six-inch platform stilettos usually reserved for bedroom performances. I retrieved them from the other end of my wardrobe and stepped on board. After briefly contemplating going downstairs without any, I rummaged in my knicker drawer and soon found exactly what I was looking for, an outrageously expensive thong that had cried "buy me" every time I walked into my favourite lingerie shop. I slipped it into position. A look over my shoulder towards the mirror confirmed the diamante T-bar was showing well above the back of the dress, just as I hoped it would be. I took hold of it and pulled it a touch higher. The fabric pulled tight against my wet pussy.

After a few dabs of perfume in strategic places, it was time to get the show on the road. Walking downstairs in stripper heels was not easy. Once I was in the hallway I could see through the glass panelled door. The coffee table had been lifted out of the way and the three of them were dancing. Carol was grinding her bum into Rob's groin. Nigel's eyes were soaking up her every wiggle.

I made my entrance.

'What do you think?' I spun full circle and threw in a booty shake for good measure.

'Gorgeous,' said Nigel with a beaming smile.

'You look like sex on legs, girl,' enthused Carol. 'There's only one way to compete with that.' Her fingers popped the first two buttons on her purple dress; her tits bulged enticingly above a matching half-cup bra. The room filled with sexual desire. I reached over to the dimmer switch and subdued the lighting.

After performing a few moves in front of him, I turned round and reversed my bum into Nigel's groin. Before long we were facing the other two, and they were facing us. At first it was all looks and little smirks. The men's hands were on our hips, both Carol and I had our hands clasped together just below our chins. Rob's eyes were drilling through my dress.

Nigel's hands were the first to wander upwards, stopping only when they were tucked in under my boobs. His thumbs then ventured a little further. I sensed his hesitation; he was testing the water, waiting to see if I would ease his arms back down with my elbows. By not doing so I gave him the green light to go further. I was in the privacy of my own home, with only my best friend and a man from the other side of the world to witness it. What harm could come of letting my husband squeeze my tits in their presence? My body tingled as he took hold of them.

And so the games began.

Rob's hands moved up, delved inside Carol's dress, and popped her tits out. It was a long time since I had seen her dark nipples. I ground my butt harder into Nigel's groin; I could feel his erection pushing between my cheeks.

'Mmm, your cock feels extra hard,' I murmured with my head tilted back.

He whispered in my ear, so close I could feel his breath on my skin. 'I want to fuck you in front of them.'

I did not answer. My mind played out a number of potential scenarios. In all of them, it was Carol and Rob who started to fuck first. We watched for a while before joining in the fun. My thoughts were interrupted by Carol revealing the lacy waistband on her panties as she undid more buttons on her dress. I started to will Rob's hand down inside those panties. I wanted to watch his hand to go to work on her pussy.

Nigel must have been thinking the same way. His right hand slipped down my body until his fingertips were stroking my pubic hair through the flimsy material covering it. I felt my face redden, and my body start to ooze lust from every pore.

Moments later Carol moved away from Rob and edged towards me. Rob stayed where he was. She crooked a finger through the straps between my boobs and guided me away from Nigel. I didn't want to go, but I did want to go. Nigel's hands were the only ones I'd granted access to my flesh in over eight years. He didn't hold on to me. He was consenting to what we both knew was about to happen. A sexual craving drove me towards Rob. I felt the heat of his body against mine, and his hard cock pressing into my back. My nipples hardened to new heights as two unfamiliar hands went on to my breasts. They felt absolutely wonderful.

Watching Nigel's hand foraging inside Carol's knickers added to my excitement. I started to pull the hem of my dress up can-can style, flashing them the shiny red triangle covering my pussy, knowing they would see how damp it was.

Our games had already taken an unexpected turn, but they took another totally unexpected one when Carol moved towards me, forcing Nigel to come with her. She lifted Nigel's hand out of her knickers and took hold of mine, guiding it towards her loins. Her hand slipped up my dress, inside my thong and down to my bush. Her eyes were telling me to reciprocate. I slid my fingers under the lacy fabric and went in search of her pubic hair. My fingertips hit the top of her moist slit without finding any. Carol smiled a cheeky smile. My middle finger was now on her engorged bud.

The men moved away. Carol's long nails started to scratch against my skin. At first I didn't like it, but as my pussy heated up, the pleasure grew. Our faces moved closer, our mouths homed in on each other. I was telling myself we were kissing and fondling each other to excite our men, but in truth, their presence was getting forgotten. Our wet tongues wrestled and danced together. It was so naughty, it was so beautiful. I became lost in the moment. A strange desire to transfer my tongue from Carol's mouth to her pussy built inside me. Her free hand went onto my breast. I mirrored her action. Our clothes had to go. Without disengaging our mouths we lowered our upper bodies. I ripped open the last two buttons on her dress. Carol yanked my thong down my thighs.

Our mouths had to part if we wanted to finish what we had started. Carol dropped her panties and kicked them off her feet. My eyes focused in on her shaven pussy as I frantically removed my thong. Carol's dress fell to the floor. She reached down to the hem of my dress and started pulling upwards. Moments later I was standing butt naked in my heels.

'Lie on the floor,' I commanded, desperately wanting to bury my face in her pussy.

Carol didn't need asking a second time. And she didn't need to be told to open her legs. I started with gentle tongue caresses on her inner thighs. The musky smell of her pussy filled my nostrils, beckoning me towards it. Next I licked her groin and succumbed to an urge to bite into her flesh. She yelped as I did so.

'Nice,' she murmured, encouraging me to devour her.

As I bit into her groins several more times, her yelps turned into soft gasps.

Deciding her clit could wait, I attacked her sopping wet pussy with my lips, and lost my tongue inside her delicious tasting cunt. Every now and then I ran my nose over her clit and on into her pussy, covering my face with her juices.

'Fingers, give me fingers,' moaned Carol's desperate voice.

I lifted my head away and took a moment to admire her pink, glistening hole. It was then that I became aware of my husband standing naked with one foot either side of her face, his cock in his hand. Carol was staring up at his balls, clearly loving the view.

With two fingers in Carol's cunt, I set my tongue to

work on her clit. The quiet squelching as I finger-fucked her was music to my ears. I was on my knees with my head between Carol's legs. A finger started to caress my vulva. I knew whose fingers they must be, Nigel had not moved. Just enjoy it, I told myself. And enjoy it I did. First one finger went into me, and then a second. Another hand delved between my thighs. I moved my knees apart to give it easier access to my clit.

If the whole situation was not wonderful enough, what happened minutes later was beyond belief.

'Can I fuck your wife?' asked Rob.

'You'd better ask her,' said Nigel's breathless voice.

There was no need to think about it. I'd already allowed Rob's fingers inside me. His cock was sure to follow, just as sure as night follows day.

'My cunt is all yours,' I declared.

His hands stretched my buttocks apart as he penetrated my vagina. His cock opened me up and pushed deep inside. The thrill of it all made me thrust my fingers in and out of Carol's cunt even faster. She responded by thrusting her hips, making it difficult for my darting tongue to stay in contact with her bud. I could only imagine what my husband was doing as I was being fucked by another man, and while I fingered and licked the pussy of the naked woman between his feet.

And then it happened; I felt Carol's vagina pulsing around my fingers. I heard the groans of absolute pleasure emanating from her mouth. It was too much, I climaxed moments later, bucking as an orgasm shot through me. Robs hands grabbed my thighs and pulled me hard onto him. His cock exploded up my cunt.

We held our positions as I gently lapped sweet tasting juices from Carol's pussy.

Rob finally pulled out. That was the cue for me to look

up. Carol had my husband's spunk all over her smiling face. It was time to grab the tissues.

In the calm after the storm, we all remained naked and I dispatched Nigel to prepare some coffee.

'Susan, can I ask you something?'

'Yes,' I said dubiously, knowing Carol only called me Susan when she was uncertain about the reply she would get.

'Would you like to watch Nigel fuck me in the arse?'

The image shot into my head. Carol bent over the armchair, Nigel pummelling her from behind.

'Do you let him do that to you?' she continued.

'Yes, sometimes.' I failed to add I had developed a penchant for A-levels over the years.

'Shall we make it happen?'

'Yes, I think he'd enjoy that.'

'But would you enjoy watching it?'

'Yes I would.' My eyes were drawn to Rob's cock. The dirty talk was making it hard again. 'Can I suck that?' I asked.

'Of course you can.'

I lowered my mouth onto his shaft. As I was bent over him, running my lips up and down his beautiful cock, I suddenly felt something cool hitting my arse crack. It soon became obvious that Carol was preparing me for what was to come, even though I had not explicitly agreed to Rob taking my arse. She even went as far as probing me with a lubricated finger. I didn't protest.

Upon hearing Nigel return with a tray of four coffees and a jug of milk, I lifted my head out of Rob's lap and smiled at my husband. 'You won't believe the treat we have in store for you.'

'Oh, what's that?' His cock twitched a little before he put the tray down on the displaced coffee table.

'Carol was wondering if you would like to do her, doggy style.'

Their eyes met and Carol teasingly moved her knees apart. He stared at her pussy as she parted her lips for him. His cock visibly hardened.

'Up the arse,' I added. 'She's already lubed up and waiting for you. Rob and I are going to watch you do it.'

Rob added a bit more filth. 'And then I'm going to fuck Susie's arse.'

'This should be good,' said Nigel enthusiastically, his cock now rock hard. 'I've always admired your backside.'

'Well, now's your chance to fuck it.' Carol rotated and dropped to her knees to the floor. Her peachy butt was begging to be taken. Even I had urges to do something obscene with it.

Nigel came up behind her and positioned the head of his cock against her hole. I could hardly believe what I was watching as he gently eased it into her anus, losing his full length inside it.

'Oooh, you feel good,' murmured Carol. 'Do me good and proper. I want to feel your spunk spurting up my arse.'

Rob grew even harder in my hand as we enjoyed every thrust, and every groan, and the delightful expressions on their faces. The sound of my husband slapping against my best friend's butt was something I never expected to listen to in a million years. I resisted temptation and avoided rubbing Rob's cock; I wanted it to stay nice and stiff for my arse.

When it was our turn, I moved the armchair I was going to bend over into the middle of the floor. As Rob took me, I moaned like a whore, and enjoyed every moment of it. If only I could have had Nigel's cock in my mouth at the same time, it would have been the magical spit roast many of my fantasies were made of.

We slept off our exertions upstairs and woke just before midday. After a cup of coffee, we hugged and kissed each other goodbye on the doorstep. Carol had to get over to her mum's for Sunday lunch. If she hadn't had to go, I fear we might have all stripped off and started fucking each other again.

Before Carol and Rob were tucking into their Sunday dinner, I'd been on the internet to book a pair of return tickets to Singapore. I'm very much looking forward to the trip, Carol says she has a few interesting friends out there, and some interesting equipment in her spare bedroom. I'm so glad I got back into my old dress. I'd forgotten just how much I love playing the slut now and then.

Party Favour
by Fierce Dolan

'Are you sure you still want to do this?' the Host asked, as he closed the door.

'Definitely,' Aja affirmed. 'I've been dying to fulfil this position since I first came to Party.' She felt quite small standing in the huge foyer of the home, but thoroughly exhilarated at having finally arrived. Aja had even lied and ditched work, cancelling the self-defence class she taught so she could devote all her energy to preparing. She wondered what Cody would think if he knew about her passion. They were getting closer lately, but she would cross that bridge when she got to it.

First thing, she'd deep conditioned her long black hair, leaving it silky soft and shiny. Half the day was spent on figuring out what to wear, though she didn't have to wear much. Aja had been paranoid that her friends, concerned for her sudden illness, would pop by to check on her, only to catch Aja tearing through piles of stockings and garter belts. In her anticipation of the event, she had taken several opportunities to pleasure herself, careful to toy only with her perpetually engorged clit, leaving her vagina tight and eagerly awaiting the evening's festivities.

But finally she had bathed, soaking in scented sudsy water. Meticulously, she removed every hair from her sex, legs and any other place where it might disrupt sensation. Finally deciding on a light peach garter belt and stockings, she thought they would provide the right balance between bare flesh and eye candy. Then throwing an ivory slip dress over them, she headed to the home of the Host.

Even though she was excited, Aja was amazed she was so calm. She didn't really know any of the guests well, though conversation and mingling was hardly the point of Party. Every now and then she recognized someone from around town as being from Party. They would exchange a knowing look, then proceed on their way. As a martial arts expert Aja was used to having interesting nuances in her life, so this wasn't really any different. Party was one, however, that she thoroughly enjoyed.

'Well, Pet' the Host responded, 'I told you I had been watching you and thought you would make a wonderful treat for Party long ago. I didn't know you were interested in Favouring until you came to me. But I must admit,' he said, looking her over as she disrobed, 'I think you will make this Party a smashing success.'

Aja smiled. In their few short conversations, she had come to like the Host quite a bit. She knew that he was honest and wouldn't have chosen her to favour his party had he not held her ability in high esteem. Even though he had no street knowledge of Aja, she knew from Party that he was a flaming bottom, and seemed to understand her desire, her need for possession and submission.

'Now,' he began, 'you remember the rules we discussed, yes?'

She nodded, squirming as she peered into the room behind him, wondering if they were alone.

'You will have a room to yourself, to which I will show you momentarily. As Host, I will be your Keeper this evening, but you will be alone with my guests, until

11 p.m. I will come for you at that time. Until then, every male who attends Party will be serviced by you.'

Aja shivered as she listened. Standing in the grand home was surreal, a Favour to Party, a dream about to come true.

'You will be the first woman that every heterosexual man here mounts, this evening. You will not be serviced by any women, or repeat services for the men, until after your Favouring time is completed. Then you may do whatever you like. Your role as Favour implies that you are here to provide a service, not to receive one. You will offer only your sex for pleasure, as there will be other Favours to provide oral and other services, as well as there will be others who service my female guests. There will be no talking during your favouring time. Favours don't speak. Understood?'

Aja nodded.

'This is a very special honour that you have been given, Pet. But I would not have chosen you for my Party, were you not perfect.'

'I know,' Aja whispered. She pursed her lips. 'Thank you.' Her heart fluttered against her ribs, a tiny bird's wings meting the moments to freedom.

'Come along now, it's almost time,' he said, motioning for her to follow.

They entered a room lavishly decorated in burgundy velvet, lighted only by a muted chandelier and candlelight reflected in many mirrors. Aja had never seen such a decadent home. It was definitely the most extravagant Party display she'd witnessed. Her breath caught as she took in all the details of the room, her room. Tingles shot through her body, her nipples awakening with the sudden chill. A large low mahogany table fitted with a plush velvet covering and pillows sat on a raised platform in the room's centre. Above the table hung two shackles, and a small gauge chain for each with black leather manacles at their free ends. Burgundy ribbons were tied at two corners of one end of the table, so that her legs could be bound.

'We have found that this sort of suspension works quite well, allowing you to stay bound yet have mobility for any position. You know, we can adjust these to fit you perfectly, so your arms don't tire,' the Host assured her, placing one of the manacles on her wrist. 'We want you to be completely comfortable in your service.'

'I don't think that will be a problem,' Aja purred, still awed at the grand preparations. It was all for her, and the hostage scenario aroused her beyond imagination. Never could she live out this desire in her private love life – whenever she had one. Who would have believed that a Wushu Master of the tenth degree black sash could need such a release? And it was mere moments away. Her heart raced with anticipation as the Host slid on the last manacle and bound each of her legs just above the knee. He bent her legs and tightened down the dark ribbons, forcing her hips to rise slightly, giving complete access to her swollen sex. He checked her positioning against the mirrors, and when he was satisfied, covered her eyes with a silk crimson scarf.

'You are a beautiful Favour,' she heard him say. 'The colours of this room set your complexion off remarkably. I chose this room just for you.' She heard a muted clap of hands, and smiled as she felt the pride radiating from her Host. 'Oh yes, I've put your things away, safely, and the stop word will be distributed to all the guests. Don't hesitate to use it if you need to.'

'Ah ... excuse me?' Aja asked, rising up a bit. 'What is the stop word for the evening?'

'Libertine,' he said. 'Use it if you need to. The stop

word rule has been well-enforced at Party. Very well, then. Our other Favours should be arriving shortly. Now where in the world are they ...' She heard him mutter as he wandered off down the hall, leaving Aja alone.

She smiled then tested her bindings. They would be easy to break in an emergency, but she foresaw no need for such. Instead, Aja continued pressing her tethers, delighting in the feel of them lightly digging into her flesh, holding her in place. She laughed to herself, almost alarmed at her lack of fear of being bound, blindfolded, and displayed. As a martial artist she had no need for fear, though it was nice to bring herself close to submission, just to be near it, to see what it would be like if it was even possible. And this was the only way. This was what she'd craved for ages, even before Party came into her life ... the revelry of being taken, over and over, no seduction, no strings, no responsibility, just sheer blissful sex.

From the first hands that grazed her inner thigh, Aja was riding waves of ecstasy. Even though her own gratification was not at the fore of the experience she revelled in the many hands, mouths, and cocks in and on her body, all at once. The attentions, the sensations bombarding her were her gratification.

She could not have foretold the excitement of being the Favour for all these men. She had been with multiple partners at Party before, but it was not like this. Nothing was like knowing you were the appetizer for a feast of orgy, that you were what whetted the guests and enticed them to devour. And Aja had no control over any of it. They approached her, some with tension in their bodies, anxiety. Maybe it was their first Party, and she was their first Favour. Maybe they'd attended many Parties and in her anticipated the glory of the evening ahead. Regardless, by the time they finished with Aja, their tension dissipated and they were fully present in the spirit of Party.

Aja could feel the eyes watching her as she was fucked, groped. Mouths ventured to her nipples, fingers, even her ears and anus. No part of her was left untouched. And with each cock, she gave a bit more, gushing wet until she could not even feel cock, only steady pounding, thighs rubbing against her own, sweaty bodies sliding. The only sounds were soft whimpers and an occasional whispered affirmation. Blind to it all, Aja let herself be skin, pussy, tight nipples, pounded and twisted until she was Party.

Cody had begun to feel guilty, somewhat, for his penchant for Party. He'd not been in the scene long and when he first started attending he was free, unfettered, no love interest. But he'd kept going despite his interest in Aja, because it had yet to pass that they would actually *be*. So he had attended a few evenings intermittently and fucked every petite Asian he could find. It was easy to get lost in the sweat-slicked bodies, the salty sweet scents, and just not think any more.

Never in his wildest dreams could Cody have envisioned something like Party, let alone experienced it. But late one night after his buddies had retired from bar hopping a beautiful woman approached him, and with no other prospects he let her bring him to Party. Even though he never saw her after that night his one foray left him with an open invitation to return to the exclusive engagement. He kept it to himself. Cody could have brought a trusted soul with him, but he knew no one he could share Party with.

As soon as he entered the home, he was surrounded by the undulating sounds of sex. He was greeted by an older man, the Host, who gave him a glass of wine and escorted him to a changing room. The Host's eyes grazed over Cody's bared form as he stripped, but he didn't mind – just part of the experience. The Host gingerly ran a finger along Cody's browned shoulder and ogled his semi-erect cock, then left Cody alone. He ran his hands over the dusting of blond hair on his chest, the charged atmosphere ghosting a tingle over his skin. He paused for a moment, glancing in the mirror as he tweaked a pink nipple between his fingers, savouring that it didn't take much for him to prepare for Party. Following the Host back down to the main floor, Cody wondered what festivities were planned. He knew to expect the basic format of each gathering, opening with a Favour and ending in divine debauchery accented, of course, with the curious flair of each Host.

The Host parted the door to a dimly lit room full of men and one young woman on a centre table. 'This is where you will start,' the Host instructed. 'After you have had my Favour, you are welcome to sample the rest of my Party.' He ushered Cody into the room, then closed the door.

Cody nodded, his attention turning back to the scene in the room. Bound was a young woman being taken from behind by a black man, someone whom Cody hadn't seen before. Another man waited near them for his turn. Cody stood back, watching the dark flesh pound into the pink sex, the contrast of their fair and mocha skin tones glistening in the candlelight. He gazed around the room at the other men, some of whom had finished and were taking in a few more minutes of the lovely affair. Others were nursing erections with their hands, having had her earlier in the evening and now returning merely to spectate. Just watching, not even engaging was intoxicating. Cody never ceased to be amazed at how the mere perception of sex, any sex, aroused him.

Groans from the dark man brought his attention back to the table, as he saw the man pull out. The man braced himself over the woman for a few seconds, then placed her on her back, kissing her belly as he walked away. When he left her, the woman's scarved face turned to blindly follow the sound of his footsteps, turning in Cody's direction.

At first he thought he was mistaken, that his penchant for placing the features of Aja on any Asian women in earshot had gotten the best of his senses. But as he moved closer to the table he saw that his eyes were not playing tricks. The body writhing under the mouth of this man did indeed bear the pouting lips of Aja, her wavy black hair, slim hips, and the perky little nose that he would know anywhere. Here, at Party, favouring all the men in this room was his darling fighting dragon.

Cody wanted to be shocked or angered to find her here. He wanted to think terrible things, but all he felt was hard and ready, and utterly, completely turned on by watching this man have his way with Aja. Had he seen her at Party before and not known it? No. It wasn't possible. He would have known. She'd never been a Favour before at any events he'd attended. And in the casual setting of the latter hours of Party, he would have seen her. Confused, Cody felt guilty for watching, for wanting, unable to do anything but stand back, mouth agape, and stroke his cock.

Before he knew it, the man reached his climax and was leaving Aja. The awkward moment of approaching her had arrived. Cody couldn't help but note the irony of his hesitation. There she was, freely offered after months of envisioning pouncing on her. But she wouldn't know it was him. He couldn't talk to her or communicate with her at all. That was *never* part of his fantasies. Cody had only ever wanted Aja, knowing that she wanted him, having her fully, knowingly all over him. Cody knew that if he broke the rules of engagement and didn't accept the Favour or attempted to talk to a Favour he would not be welcomed back to Party. Doing so might even endanger Aja's future invitations, as well. But what could he do? There were already men waiting to have her after him, and he would not gain entrance to the rest of the soirée if he eluded his gracious Host's Favour.

He stepped up to the platform, walking to her side first, taking in her nude form. Her body was marked from recreation of the evening, from all the men at Party. Her lips were swollen, reddened from harsh lustful kisses, and her nipples purpled from calloused hands. He ran his fingers down the length of Aja's body and she instinctively moved toward his touch. He spread her legs wide, revelling in her brazen will to be publicly bound, splayed, and fucked. Her sex was completely bare, even its inner lips exposed. Her crotch was a pool of liquids and he traced his fingers in the crease of her inner thigh, staring at her pussy. At his lingering touch the tip of her tongue outlined her bottom lip then retreated back into her mouth. Affirmed in her lust, Cody pulled her toward him so that her bottom was past the edge of the table. Cody sucked in his breath, placed one hand on her abdomen, and with one hard shove, pushed completely inside.

With a jolt, Aja's heels dug into the soft coverlet beneath her bringing her back from her trance. Suddenly she was aware that someone was taking her, pushing in. She could feel cock prodding deep into her cunt, the tip making full contact with the crown of her cervix, completely filling her. She would have thought it impossible to detect specific features of anything placed inside her at this point, but indeed, the cock in her now was filling her thoroughly, stretching her more amply than the multitude of men who had preceded it. She could feel him pressing sensitive areas she'd not been conscious of after the first few guests' ministrations.

Aja was incredibly aroused, not just from the treatment she'd received all evening, submitting to the wants and uses of the guests, but from the insanely glorious rubbing of the cock in her. She could feel the body of the man low over her, his nipples rubbing hers as they fucked. His breath came warm on her neck, his hands cupping her buttocks, lifting, holding her in position to pull out and then surge completely within her with each stroke. When he slowed the pace Aja went limp in his arms, completely hanging on his every movement. He began to fuck her more slowly, more thoroughly, so that his cock never lost contact with the sensitive folds deep inside.

He fucked her masterfully, as if it was his will was to drive her insane, as if he knew exactly how she wanted to be taken. She could feel him watching her, his face hovering just above hers. Aja hung clinging to every stroke, praying he wouldn't move, wouldn't shift his weight even the slightest little bit. She wasn't supposed to be feeling. She was just supposed to be, not taking anything for herself.

And then, before her mind could register what was happening, she was shuddering. His arms came around her waist, holding her in the climax, exquisitely fucking her, so that his every gesture brought her pleasure. In her delirium, she could hear the activity of the men in the room crescendo, languid movements all around her. Fevered moans resonated low and primal until Aja realised she was hearing her own voice, her throat opening, giving way to a wild deep groan as her pussy tightened and contracted. Seconds later the man driving her came, each of his slowing movements bringing him to rest lower and lower on her chest until his dampened forehead cradled on her shoulder. He laid on her a few more seconds then pulled out, leaving Aja completely sated, trembling and empty.

Aja drifted in and out as the remaining men took Favour, but none of them regaled her like the man who had left her spent. She was aware of their presence, sometimes even feeling them in her. Mostly, she just lay back, peacefully receiving them. She lost all track of time, and succumbed to the men of Party.

When the Host finally came for her, he allowed her to collect herself a bit, then showed her into an adjoining bath where attendants helped her freshen up. They soothed her reddened skins with cool moist cloths, rubbing scented oils into the areas bitten with marks from the manacles and ribbon. She nibbled sweet fruits as they pulled and kneaded her flesh, fuelling her with revitalizing energy.

'Our guests have been well pleased with your service, Pet,' the Host told her, a hint of pride gleaming in his eyes. 'If you ever wish to Favour again, Miss, it would be my honour to have you.' With those words, he kissed her lightly on the cheek, bowed to her, and motioned her out the door.

He led her back down the main hall to a huge drawing room, which held a vast array of candelabras. Bodies writhed, copulating in every fashion, all around. This was a more familiar scene of Party to Aja. She entered the room, the other Favours already receiving overtures from the guests. For the first time since the evening began, she felt somewhat self-conscious, wondering if the man who had so artfully and wilfully possessed her watched her now.

She was immediately pulled into the arms of two women, who pushed her back on to the floor, covering her with kisses. Trails of moisture cooled where their lips passed over. A lovely brunette lapped at her cunt, giving the long-needed attention that her clit had been craving. Tired of being on her back, Aja rose into the midst of their heap, and grabbed the cute redhead, gently, deftly turning her on her back. Surrendering to her own need for closeness, Aja lavished long kisses on the woman, the essence of semen and other women awakening her taste buds. She loved being with women, and in her favouring time had forgotten how much she looked forward to her secret interludes with them at Party. In seconds she tasted the sweet cunt, savouring the delicateness of the flesh and the whimpers rising from the creature in her hands. The brunette had taken station at Aja's sex, wedging herself under Aja's bottom, so that Aja was fully seated on the woman's face. So intent on her was Aja that she gave not another thought to the male guests.

The attention that the blonde was giving his cock didn't have nearly as much to do with Cody's heightened arousal as the scene that played out a few feet from him. He'd no idea that Aja enjoyed women, and he added that to his slowly growing list of interests he didn't know she had. He longed to walk away from the mouth that was swallowing his cock, though he knew that to do so would not only be in poor taste, but would disrupt the entourage that was pleasuring Aja. Cody was wholly mesmerized by the sight.

His breath had caught when she had first emerged from the dark hallway on the arm of the Host, and he was torn between running away and to her. But he was in it so deep he couldn't get away, even if he had truly wanted to. Before Party's end, Aja would know he was there, and that he, along with all the other so-inclined men, had sexed her.

He let the woman satisfy her oral needs with his cock, but before she could grow concerned for his lack of climax, he turned her sex to his, taking her from behind. Trying to keep his attention on the woman, to give her some sort of gratification for choosing him to couple, Cody found that he was still sidetracked despite the tight heat of his charge's orgasms. It was Aja he fixated on, now engaging the two women and a man. It was a beautiful thing, observing her climax. Even though his cock was buried in another woman, he watched Aja come again from the other man's penetration, his own cock twitching with the memory of her cunt clutching at him. He chided himself for attempting to trick himself into thinking that the women he fucked at Party were Aja.

When another man expressed interest in the woman he was mating, Cody took the opportunity to approach Aja. She was still on her hands and knees from her last tryst, her beautiful bottom facing him. Without as much as a hint of his presence, he mounted her, her breath hitching somewhat, hips sinking into a rhythm of recognition. All of Cody's resolve melted into the sweet pussy on his cock, as it pumped him. Aja was fucking him, her body sitting back on him further with each stroke. She still didn't know him, but clearly she knew his cock.

Aja couldn't believe what she was feeling. He had been

watching her. Not only had he been watching, but he dared take her again, anonymously. She delighted in the game, but not nearly as much as she did the huge cock that remembered exactly how to stroke her. Already, she was nearing orgasm, and though her will compelled her to see this man, her body was rooted, wanting more.

Before she could resist though, strong arms lifted her, not quite extracting the member from her, turning her on to her back. In a split second, there she was, face-to-face with her secret lover, and her heart's desire – Cody Baptiste.

Her first response was panic, and she scrambled to pull away ... except she didn't want to. What could she do? They were surrounded on all sides by people who thrived on innominate presence at Party. She couldn't draw attention to themselves, or anyone. Her mind raced. *Cody* was the one who had best topped her, the only one that made her come, and the last person she expected to see at Party. Her hand came to her mouth, reality setting in, and she looked around to see if anyone had noticed their subtle commotion. But no one had. No aspect of Party had been disturbed. There was only Cody, not speaking, just looking down at her with understanding in his eyes, his cock still sheathed in her cunt.

'Shhh,' he whispered. 'It's all right,' he chanted into her ear, continuing to fuck her, nipping her neck and earlobes. After a few minutes, she relaxed back into his cadence, knotting her ankles around his hips, moving with him.

'I wanted to tell you it was me,' he whispered, 'but I couldn't ...'

'I understand,' she said. 'We would have broken a rule ...' She paused on the words, wondering what he thought of her for wanting Party. 'I liked it, Cody ... I've never felt anything like that before ...'

'I couldn't believe it was you,' he agreed. 'It was a dream come true.'

'Really?' she fretted. They had stopped moving and talked softly. 'I don't know how to explain this ...'

'You don't have to,' Cody interrupted. 'I'm kinda relieved, actually, that you ... that you're here.'

With that Aja pulled him to her, and exerting just a bit of Wushu strength, flipped him beneath her. She rode him hard, pinning his arms to the floor, and eked out another orgasm. His cock was absolutely delicious, the way it filled and claimed her. Holding his arms firmly in place, she leaned into him, her breasts swaying above his lips. She rose and sat hard on his cock over and over, until he released in her.

'So ... I guess we have no more little secrets,' Aja said.

Nodding, Cody smiled at her. 'Maybe we could make this a joint venture ... next time?'

'Next time?' Aja asked, perking up ...

Tied Up in Knots
by Antonia Adams

Consciousness returned slowly. But for a few seconds Will thought he must still be dreaming. He couldn't move. He couldn't see much either, on account, he realised slowly, of the blindfold wrapped around his eyes. He was lying face-down on what he was pretty sure was his own bed. The familiar scent of him was on the sheets. He was buck naked. His arms and legs were tied. Both his hands were straight up in front of him, his legs were spread-eagled.

He tested the bonds. Something metallic secured his hands to the bedstead. Something softer, but quite strong, held his ankles apart. There was a dry, slightly bitter taste in his mouth and his head felt fuzzy.

Sara, he remembered hazily, had said something about tying him up being her ultimate fantasy. But how long ago had that been? He didn't have any memory beyond them having drinks in his lounge just after dinner. Hang about – they'd brought the wine into the bedroom. She'd been giggling, waving a pair of handcuffs around that she'd borrowed from work.

'Put your uniform on and you can do what you like to me.' He'd remembered saying that as he sprawled out on the bed. God she was hot – even without her uniform – especially without her uniform. She had tits to die for and she always wore tops that were too tight so he could see every curve, see the perky outline of her nipples.

He was getting hard just thinking about it. But where was she? The last thing he remembered was her smile and her dark hair falling forward onto his naked chest.

'Sara?' He moved his head enough to yell, surprised to find his voice was slurred. They hadn't had that much to drink, had they?

He wasn't really expecting an answer. He was almost sure he was alone. The room had a silence about it – an emptiness. Shit!

'Sara!' he called again. Maybe she'd just popped out to get more wine or something.

No, she hadn't. She wouldn't leave him trussed up helpless and go out. Would she?

How long had he been lying here anyway? Something told him it had been a while. More than a while. He ached with the unnatural position.

Then he remembered with a cold little chill the discussion they'd had earlier that evening …

'You want to shag Julie? Am I hearing this right – you want to shag my best friend?'

'No, I didn't say that. I said Peter had mentioned they'd sometimes messed about with other couples. That was all I said. Hey – don't get so stressed, babe.'

'You said she had nice breasts.'

'Well, – yeah, she does, but that doesn't mean I want to shag her.'

'You said she had nice breasts and they sometimes messed about with other couples – what else could you mean exactly?'

'I meant nothing, babe. I meant nothing – OK.'

He didn't know how he'd got into that conversation.

Sara was gorgeous but she was jealous as hell. She'd told him once before what she'd do to him if she ever caught him being unfaithful. It involved some pretty sadistic stuff.

There was no doubt in his mind she'd do it either. She'd been involved in a bit of a scene when he'd met her; with some pretty dodgy people. Jesus, why had he opened his mouth before he'd got his brain into gear?

He thought he'd smoothed things over, but maybe he hadn't. A little slick of fear ran down his back. Maybe this was her idea of revenge – tying him up and leaving him, helpless and naked in his own flat. Yeah, that was definitely the sort of thing that would appeal to Sara. There had always been a touch of the dominatrix about her. It was one of the things that had quite turned him on. But he didn't know about doing it for real.

From outside the room there was a click of sound. A door closing somewhere. He strained his ears, his senses on full alert. There was a rustling, as though someone had taken off a coat and then footsteps coming across the wooden floor in the hall towards the bedroom door. Steady, measured footsteps, someone wearing flat shoes. Sara had been wearing heels – he was sure she'd been wearing heels. Maybe she'd taken them off.

A breath of air swept across his back and he knew someone had opened the bedroom door.

'OK, babe, enough's enough. You've had your fun – untie me please.'

No answer. The bed dipped beneath someone's weight. He had a sudden terrible vision of it being his cleaner. She had her own key. Could he have slept through the night? Surely not. Anyway she'd hardly just sit on the bed. She'd say something like, 'Sorry, Will, didn't realise you were in,' in that breathy little-girl-voice she had, and then she'd close the door.

Not much shocked Carol.

The person on the bed still didn't speak, but he could hear breathing. The soft edge of a finger ran down his spine from his neck to the top of his buttocks, then paused. He shivered, and immediately wished he hadn't. There was no sense in letting her know she'd got to him. She knew he wasn't a fan of these power games. Well, not when he was the one tied up anyway.

The finger resumed its gentle stroking. The finger became a hand, soft and smooth with long nails that scraped slightly. It had to be Sara. He breathed in, trying to catch the scent of her, but all he got was the faint smell of soap.

The hand morphed into two hands that rubbed and stroked his shoulders, circled the muscles below, moved down his back and finally came to rest on his buttocks; paused before pulling them gently apart.

Another little shift in weight. Another sound somewhere in the room, but before he had time to consider the significance of this the soft wetness of a tongue circled his arsehole.

Holy shit. He was suddenly more aroused than he'd ever been in his life. If this was submission, he was up for it. One hundred and ten per cent totally up for it. In fact, why the hell hadn't they done it before? He arched back to meet the tongue, wanting it to go further, wanting more.

The tongue probed him, flicking and teasing, darting in and out, a soft little harbinger of joy. Then just as suddenly as it started it was replaced by a finger. He couldn't believe the sensations as the finger pushed slowly in. He groaned.

At the same moment the hands started up again on his shoulders, rubbing, smoothing, circling, pummelling. Round and round, over and across his skin.

The significance of this didn't hit him straight away. And then it did – smashing into him like a bucket of ice. If Sara was massaging his shoulders, who the hell had their finger up his arse?

He jumped away, his sphincter muscles tightening round the finger, but not managing to expel it.

There was a soft laugh from the door. Sara's laugh.

'Enjoying it, Will? Enjoying your spot of swapping are you?'

'Jesus Christ, Sara ...' He reared up against his bonds. But he had no chance of getting away. 'At least take the blindfold off,' He was trying not to beg. 'At least let me see ...'

'Who's got their finger up your arse?' Her laugh tinkled out. 'Worried it might be Peter, are you?'

It could be Peter. Shit! He could have another man's finger up his arse. He still had a raging hard on. Double shit. Did that make him bi like Peter? Not that there was anything wrong with being bi. He just – well – he just would have liked more say in the matter, that was all.

'Maybe you'd like a cock up your arse.' She was coming across the room. Her mocking voice was right by his ear. 'That could be arranged.'

'I don't want a cock up my arse,' he said quietly. Not sure it was the right thing to say. Not sure if it was even true. The finger was still there. He had the biggest hard on in history. He wasn't sure what he wanted any more.

'Take the blindfold off.'

'What's the magic word?' She scraped a nail down his back and he flinched.

'Take the fucking blindfold off,' he said in a fit of

bravado.

'Wrong answer, Will.'

There was ice in her voice. He could feel his bravado slipping away. That probably hadn't been the brightest move he'd ever made. He was, after all, totally at her mercy. And whoever else was in the room. He wasn't even sure it was Peter and Julie.

What if it was someone from her past? She'd been texting a lot earlier. He hadn't taken much notice – she couldn't survive without texting her mates.

Sara had been into all sorts when he'd met her. It was one of the things that had attracted him. The danger, the edge.

He was on the edge now all right.

The finger was removed. He sighed. Ground his pelvis into the sheets. He was half disappointed.

'Maybe we shouldn't do this?' That was Peter's voice. It seemed to have come from the direction of his head. So he hadn't had a man's finger up his arse. Well, that was something.

'No, you shouldn't be doing it,' he decided to appeal to his friend's better nature. 'Untie me, mate, can you?'

'But it's your ultimate fantasy – a foursome with you helpless and bound.' Julie's voice was breathy, excited. Julie was the owner of the finger. Now, she dropped a kiss on his arsehole and cupped his balls with her hand. Which was pretty exciting in itself, he had to admit.

'And you haven't said the safe word, Will. We'd stop if you said the safe word.'

What bloody safe word.

'I think he wants a bit of cock,' Sara said evilly. 'How about it, darling?' He felt her nail again. A casual scrape down his spine, digging in a little between his buttocks, toying with his arsehole. Jesus, why the hell was he so turned on?

How could he hate her and want her so much in the same breath?

Now she was between his legs squeezing something cold against his crack, lubing him up with her fingers and his body wanted it – despite everything he'd ever known about himself – all the preconceptions he'd ever had, his mind was as open as his body to the invasion. His mind welcomed it, longed for it.

He wanted cock. He wanted a rock hard shaft of man-meat up his arse.

'Are you sure he's up for this?'

'Course he is.' Sara's voice was pure darkness.

A little moan escaped him. She was right. He did want it. He was rearing up, almost on his knees, pushing back against the hardness that was pressing against his sphincter. There were cool hands around his dick – foreign fingers, Julie's fingers again, stroking his balls, pumping him up and down, but it wasn't the fingers he wanted, it was invasion.

And as the hardness pushed in – a sweet explosion of pain – he yelled out but he also arched back to meet it. Who'd have thought it felt so good to have a dick up his arse. He'd never realised they were so bloody hard – so rock-like, so good. He breathed, gasped, yelped, quivered, existed in a red mist of ecstasy.

Julie's fingers were jerking him off in perfect rhythm to the pounding his backside was taking. He was beyond thought now – beyond everything he'd ever known – as he gave himself up to the pleasure pain of what was happening.

His body betrayed him. He couldn't stop himself. He was coming and coming and coming. He thought it would never stop, spurt after spurt after spurt, bursting out of him, soaking the sheets. A never ending stream of jism.

The cock eased out of him. More gently than it had gone in. The hands left his balls. For a few long moments he was untouched. Unravelled. Undone. After the red heat of his orgasm he floated in a white haze of contentment.

Then, to his surprise someone was untying him, taking off the blindfold. It was Peter, he realised, as he blinked in the light. His head still felt groggy. Even though he was free he didn't feel like moving far. He stretched his cramped limbs and rolled over onto his side. It was like waking up in a porn movie.

Peter was naked, his cock semi erect. It was huge. Had he really had that up his arse? Julie, clad only in a thong, was smiling as she lay alongside him. Her breasts were now against his chest, her nipples very large very pink.

Sara was standing at the foot of the bed, naked but for her long black boots and an inscrutable little smile on her lips.

'You're a man of hidden depths,' Julie said, kissing him on the mouth.

'Not so hidden,' he said ruefully.

She giggled again. 'We were totally amazed when Sara told us your ultimate fantasy. Me and Peter – well we both thought you were a bit straight to be honest.'

'Just goes to show,' he murmured, taking advantage of the fact that her breasts were so close and bending to suck on a nipple, which peaked satisfyingly beneath his tongue.

'Naughty boy wants some more,' she squeaked.

'Well, the night is yet young.' Sara's voice had a little edge to it. 'None of us are getting up early tomorrow, are we?'

'Never get up in the morning if you can get up in the evening,' Peter said, 'That's my motto.'

Will had a feeling it might be his too. His dick was

already stirring again. Not quite ready for round two, but certainly not averse to the idea of more action shortly.

'So what other little fantasies have you got then, lover boy?' Julie murmured. 'Anything else we can help you out with?'

'Well, I've always fancied watching two women go down on each other,' Will said, giving her nipple a tweak. 'And maybe a bit more arse action, but with you girls on the receiving end this time. And us boys dishing it out.'

'A man after my very own heart,' Julie, said licking her lips.

Will glanced across at Sara. She wasn't looking quite so pleased with herself now it seemed her little plan had backfired. What had she expected? Obviously for him not to have enjoyed himself quite so much. Perhaps she'd expected him to have crawled away in embarrassment when her little games had reached their sick conclusion.

He grinned lazily at her. 'You up for that, babe? Or have you had your fill of fun and games for the night?'

He got off the bed and strolled across. His legs still felt a little shaky but his dick had recovered, it seemed. 'I assume you don't want to let our friends go home unsatisfied.'

'I'm up for anything,' she said tightly.

And he thought – no, not quite anything. He'd just twigged that he hadn't had Peter's cock up his arse. She hadn't been quite up to conning his bisexual mate into buggering him without his consent. Although she'd wanted him to think that's what had happened. No wonder it had felt so hard. The top drawer of his dressing table wasn't quite closed. The buckle from a strap-on was in the way, stopping it from shutting properly. He'd glimpsed it as he'd gone past. And it hadn't been in there earlier.

Julie had been right. He had always been straight laced in bed – a vanilla kind of man – flirting with the idea of a foursome, but never quite thinking he'd really do it.

But his game-playing girlfriend had opened a whole new Pandora's box of fetishes with her invented fantasies and her invented safe word – not to mention whatever she'd spiked his drink with to get him tied up to the bed in the first place.

He grinned, as he slid his fingers down the curve of her beautiful stomach and then jammed them up hard between her legs.

Will had a feeling it wasn't going to be quite so easy to close the Pandora's Box as it had been to open it.

Rockin' It Old School
by Lynn Lake

'Hey, where ya goin', Hailey?' Eugene yelled. He struck a chord on his Wal-Mart electric guitar, caught his pick in the steel strings and almost snapped a finger off.

'Yeah, woz up, Ha-Lo?' Myron shouted. He tried to rat-a-tat-ting a rimshot, but the drumsticks jumped out of his sweaty hands and clattered to the concrete floor of his parents' garage.

Hailey Logan just shook her head in disgust and kept right on walking, down the driveway and out on to the sidewalk, headed for downtown.

She'd been playing with Eugene and Myron – The X-urbanites, as Eugene called them – for two months now, and it was obvious to the music-serious eighteen-year-old that they were going nowhere. The two boys were more interested in getting into her pants than getting any better, or any gigs. And she'd found out from personal experience that they were just as inept in that department as they were in making music.

Hailey knew she didn't have the diva-licious good looks of a Mariah Carey or Faith Hill – with her dark hair and dark eyes, pale skin and small breasts and tiny, sinewy body, she was more punk than princess – but she had the drive and ambition, and a pretty good set of pipes.

The bell rang over the door as she pushed her way into

Second Notes, the used CD and vinyl record store on 10th Street. The owner, Gil Mendez, looked up from the pile of Alan Sherman albums an old geezer was trying to sell him and nodded at Hailey. She nodded back.

'You used to have a band, didn't you, Mr Mendez?' she asked, after the old guy had left with some money for the track.

Gil shifted the dusty stack of records to one side of the cluttered glass counter and smiled at the small girl with the soulful brown eyes. 'Now who told you that?'

Hailey shrugged her bony shoulders. 'Uh, I just heard it somewhere, I guess – you know, on the street.'

'Amber Trails? I doubt they ever heard of me out there.' He laughed and put his hands down on the counter, gazing at Hailey.

Dressed in a pair of black and white sneakers, black jeans and a black tank-top emblazoned with *Groupie* in white letters, her eyes rimmed with black eyeliner, the girl looked like a Goth skater chick. She was in the store just about every second day since school had ended, but they'd never really talked much. What's a 45-year-old ex-rocker-turned-store-owner have in common with a teenage girl? Well, maybe the music, Gil thought to himself, as he scratched his goatee and eyed Hailey's tight little bod.

She brushed some jet-black hair away from her earnest face and said, 'I know you do some, like, voice coaching or something, right? When you aren't working here.'

Gil grunted. 'You've done your homework, kid.'

Hailey's eyes flashed. 'I'm no kid, Mr Mendez. I'm gonna be the lead singer in a band – a good band. My band.' She simmered for a moment, then quickly cooled down again, smiling shyly at the man. 'Would you mind, like, listening to my voice – gimme your professional opinion or whatever?'

Gil glanced around the empty store. 'Well ... it gets pretty busy here on a Monday,' he joked. 'I don't want to lose any business.'

Hailey spun around and ran down an aisle, plucked a record out of the "D" section of Rock n' Roll and raced back up to the counter. 'I'll buy this from you – if you listen to me,' she gasped, slapping the album down on the counter.

It was She-Devil, from The Donnybrooks – Gil's old band. He grinned and said, 'OK, I'll listen.'

'You've got to get more growl into the low notes, put more belly into it.' Gil got off the couch and in behind Hailey. He coiled an arm around the teenager's tiny waist and pressed his flattened hand into her stomach, up against her diaphragm. 'Bring it up from down here – where the soul lives.'

They were in the living room of his small apartment in back of the store. Hailey had been belting out one of her own angst-heavy compositions – A Student, A-Hole. She didn't just rip off other people's music, like all those American Idol wannabes.

She felt Gil's warm, strong hand against her tummy, and the butterflies inside really started to flutter. The man's spicy aftershave, the heat from his body so close made her dizzy. He might be a dinosaur of rock, but he was still kind of cute – in a younger Cheech Marin sort of way.

'Try it again,' Gil instructed, pressing against the girl's rapidly rising and falling stomach.

Hailey cleared her throat and tried to focus, brought up a note that squeaked like a rusty mouse. She flinched, and her bum bumped Gil's groin. She felt something hard and growing harder, and she wiggled her bum just a bit, a smile spreading across her face, her body surging with heat.

'Uh, maybe we better pick this up tomorrow,' Gil said, cautious, responsible adult that he was now.

'Sure, Mr Mendez, whatever you say,' the precocious teenager breathed, snuggling in closer. The man's hot breath flooded her bare neck and shoulders, warming her up even more.

She wagged her bum against his jeaned hard-on, polishing it harder still, and she felt his hands go damp on her tummy – hot and damp, like her cunny. She shivered with excitement, her head spinning and body brimming.

'Y-yeah, OK, we'll pick it up tomorrow,' Gil mumbled.

But he didn't let go of the girl. In fact, he squeezed her tighter, pushing his cock firmly in between her taut butt cheeks. He brought his other hand around and onto her stomach, nuzzling her shiny hair. She smelled fresh and innocent and scrubbed clean, and he began moving his hips, pumping his pulsating cock into her mounded bottom.

'Mmm,' Hailey murmured, tilting her head back on to the man's shoulder, her body crackling like a plugged-in amp.

Gil peeled his hands off her tank-top and slid them in underneath the garment, over her bare, heated skin and up on to her bare breasts. 'Yes!' Hailey yelped, shuddering at his touch. He ground his cock into her ass, squeezing her cupcakes.

Hailey's boobs tingled wickedly under Gil's groping hands, her nipples jumping out and thickening. And when he bit into her neck, shivers raced up and down her spine and all through her. She'd never been so turned-on, so tuned in to a man in all her young life. He was playing her like a fine instrument, with all the skills of a virtuoso.

Gil urgently kneaded Hailey's pudding-cup breasts, fingering her obscenely elongated nipples, licking and kissing and biting her neck, head full of her dewy fragrance. His cock was a pulsing slab of meat against her rear-end, desperately seeking to burst free of its jeaned confines and dive into the superheated pink sleeve of her teen pussy.

'Fuck me, Mr Mendez!' Hailey squealed, right on the same wavelength. 'Please, fuck me!'

He quickly released her tits and pulled back and fumbled his pants open, shoving them and his boxers down. As Hailey wriggled out of her own jeans. She slid her white cotton panties over the gleaming, ivory hills of her smooth buttocks and peeked over her shoulder at Gil's twitching erection pointing directly at her. Her eyes widened – she'd never seen one *that* big before.

He was about to spin her around and throw her down on to the couch when she suddenly grabbed onto his straining dong and yanked him close, his boiled-up cap indenting the flesh of her butt cheek. 'Jesus!' he grunted, his cock jumping in the girl's damp little hand.

Gil let Hailey awkwardly tug on his pole for a moment, his body temperature soaring like a screaming guitar solo. Then he brushed her hand away and swung his dong in between her skinny legs, rubbed her pussy with it. The dark, springy fur of her cooch cushioned his sawing dick, moistened it, driving him wild.

Hailey shivered with desire and spread her trembling legs further apart. And Gil bent at the knees and speared his prick upwards, jamming his bloated cockhead into her slick petals.

'Oh, yes, please,' Hailey cried, falling back against the

man. 'Fuck me with your big, hard cock, Mr Mendez!'

Gil shoved his hips up and forward, sliding shaft into the quivering teen. He bumped against her bum, buried to the bone, tight and wet and hot. He pushed her tank-top up and clutched her exposed titties, mauling them, pumping his hips, fucking the juicy teenager.

Hailey floated on to her tip-toes and arched her back against the hard-breathing man, grabbing on to his moving hips from behind, lit up like a concert stadium, shaking like an out-of-control Beatles fan. Her cunny burned with a wonderful, full-up sensation she'd never felt before, the man's pistoning dick plugging her full of sexual electricity. Her little boobs bounced in his big hands, her nipples buzzing, her whole cock-rocked body shimmering. This was the real thing; this was what sex was supposed to be all about – raw and hot and wild, like the pulse-pounding beat of a soul-tingling song that stripped all emotions bare.

Gil thrust harder, faster, splashing against Hailey's rippling bum, fucking the girl with an intensity that shocked and shattered her, surprised even him. 'I'm coming,' he hollered into her reddened ear, pounding her pussy. 'I'm going to come inside of you!'

'Yes! Yes!' Hailey sang out, sweet orgasm welling up from her stuffed cunny and flooding her body with bliss.

Gil slammed her in a final frenzy, his churning cock getting doused with her gushing juices. Then he jerked, his cock erupting, blasting semen. He was jolted with ecstasy over and over, spurting a sticky love song deep into the crying-with-joy teen.

Hailey inspired Gil, with her voice and body and boundless enthusiasm and determination. He let her talk him into digging his old Fender Stratocaster out of the closet, arrange a jam session with his old drummer from high school days.

Tim "Stickman" Stadler was as thin and wired as ever, despite a mundane career as manager of a fast food outlet. He took one look at Hailey, heard her kitten-hiss out a dick-stiffening rendition of *Hit Me With Your Best Shot*, and was back in the band.

Their first gig was the Red Lantern Motor Inn on Main Street. Not exactly Wembley Stadium, or even House of Blues, but a start. It was a paying gig, the first of its kind for Hailey. And the eager 18-year-old was keyed up tighter than the skin on a snare drum.

'Do I look OK, Gil, Tim?' she asked for the tenth time, flipping down the visor and peering at herself in the mirror.

They were in Gil's van, heading for the Red Lantern, the two men cool as Bon Jovi on his steel horse, the girl as jumpy as Jimmy Page's fingers on a double neck. Gil and Tim were casually dressed in jeans and T-shirts, while Hailey was tarted up like a video vixen in a short, black leather skirt and a black, tummy-bearing halter top, a pair of black, spike-heeled leather boots. She'd painted on enough eyeliner to make Avril Lavigne blush, and her lips glowed with more gloss than Beyonce's, her black hair shimmering like the night.

'You look great,' Gil reminded her. He twisted his head around and grinned at Stickman.

'Really great,' Tim agreed.

Hailey started flying through some voice exercises, and the two men shook their heads. It was still an hour-and-a-half to show time. But they'd had a little experience with high-strung young girls – back in the day. Gil pulled off the road and into the empty parking lot of a city park.

'Hey, whatcha doin'?' Hailey squealed. 'We gotta get to the Red Lantern.'

'We've got to get you calmed down, first,' Gil said, turning off the motor.

Hailey stared at him. 'What're you gonna do?'

'It's not what *I'm* going to do – it's what *we're* going to do,' Gil said, nodding at Tim. 'There's no "I" in band, remember.'

He spun around in his captain's chair and took Hailey's hand, pulled her into the back of the van, Tim crouching ahead of them.

'Let's see if we can't drain off just a little of all that nervous energy,' Gil said. He sat down on the leather couch that lined one side of the converted cargo van, next to Tim. The band mates then unzipped their jeans and let it all hang out, rock-star-style, semi-hard and getting harder.

Hailey dropped to her bare knees on the foam-rubber bedlining, desperate to play the roll of the seasoned band slut. She crawled in between the two slumped men and boldly grabbed a cock in each hand.

Gil grinned, Tim grunted, as she pumped their cocks to rock-hard with her hot little sweaty hands. She'd never ever felt up two pricks at once before, but the throbbing feel of the men's dongs in her hands, the way she could make them respond to her, filled the young woman with an awesome sense of power and maturity well beyond her years. She wet her panties – in a womanly way.

Gil groaned and grabbed at her hair, as she encircled the furry base of his cock with her fingers and pulled it upright, leaned forward and dropped her shiny lips over top of his mushroomed hood. She tugged on his knob, then shook her head free and sucked up Tim's cap.

The balding man dug his fingers into the couch,

watching the excited teen slurp on the tip of his dick, feeling the incredible warmth and wetness of her lips and mouth all through his wiry body. Feeling the awful emptiness and pulsing yearning when she popped his gleaming hood out of her mouth and swallowed Gil's microphone bulb again.

Gil pushed her head down, forcing Hailey to take more of his pipe into her mouth. Which she did readily, meeting the man's stiff challenge, inhaling half his prick. She pulled up, then plummeted back down again, working his long, hard cock like she worked scales – up and down, repeatedly. He pumped his hips, fucking her wet-hot mouth, matching her sucking rhythm perfectly.

Hailey sucked on Tim's fat prick, gulping the stubby tool right down to its blonde roots before spitting it back up again. She was a girl on fire, the taste of man-meat and precome and power driving her wild. She bounced her head back and forth between the two squirming men, cheeks billowing and throat working, wet-vaccing their vein-popped dongs. The rush was amazing, her body and cunny flushing with humid heat.

'You've played us,' Gil finally intervened, as Hailey nuzzled Tim's pubes, the thin man's entire drumstick buried in the steamy cauldron of her mouth. 'Now it's time we play you.'

Hailey stared at him, not exactly sure what he meant, but sure ready to try anything.

She disgorged Tim's dripping prick and they all quickly stripped out of their clothes. Gil then lay down on his back on the floor of the van. He pulled Hailey down on top of him, catching onto her waist with one hand and steering his prong into her soaking cun with the other. She gasped when he penetrated her, groaned as he lowered her fully down onto his pole.

'That feels sooo good,' she murmured. Then started bouncing her bum up and down, fucking herself on Gil's cock.

'It's going to feel even better,' he gritted, hands riding her hips. 'Hit it, Stickman.'

Tim crouched in behind Hailey, while Gil held the girl steady. The drummer spread her butt cheeks apart and lubed up her crack. Hailey quivered like a tuning fork at the touch of the man's wet fingers in her bum cleavage, thrilled at the pressure of his thick knob against her virgin bumhole.

'Fuck my butt, Tim,' she heard herself whisper, leaning forward and grabbing on to the hair on Gil's chest.

Tim sucked some heated air into his lungs, his knees shaking, pressing, pressing the beefy head of his cock into the teenager's tender butt pucker. Hailey bit her lip and held her breath, clawing at Gil's chest, the pressure building and building. The only thing missing, to heighten the wicked sexual tension and anticipation even more, was a drum roll.

Tim popped Hailey's anal cherry and sank inside her ass, slow and sure and sensual. Hailey full-body shuddered, two grown men buried inside her now – one in the cunny and one in the bum.

'Geez, is she ever tight,' Tim wheezed. Sweat poured off the guy's bony face as he slowly moved his locked-down cock back and forth in Hailey's gripping chute.

'You got that right,' Gil agreed from down below, sliding his cock in and out of Hailey's sucking pussy.

The two band members pumped their lead singer's two sexholes in perfect harmony, grunts and groans and girlish moans filling the breathless interior of the rocking van. Hailey clung to Gil's chest, swirled her cherry-red tongue around his outstretched tongue, her stretched-out pussy and ass on fire, the smack of the men's bodies against her bum and thighs sweet, sweaty music to her burning ears.

Gil grasped the teen's jumping titties and thrust wildly into her twat, his balls boiling out-of-control. 'Here I come!' he bellowed, blowing hot, salty notes up Hailey's cooch.

Tim strangled the girl's waist and frantically slammed into her vice-like ass, his cock detonating on cue with his band mate's. His skinny body shook on the end of Hailey's trembling bum, as he hit just the perfect beat, creaming her chute with white-hot spunk.

Hailey whipped her head from side-to-side like Joplin at fever pitch, going into meltdown as the thundering cocks blasted her with liquid heat. The biggest, highest-pitched orgasm of her young sexual life crescendoed up from her prick-stuffed cunny and washed over her bloated, violated bum, rolling through her vibrating body and rocking her to the core.

The gig at the Red Lantern was a huge success, confirming Hailey's belief that she'd made the right move hooking up with Gil and Tim. Mature guys really knew how to rock it – old school, she happily thought to herself, as she jumped into the motel's private hot tub for a post-concert celebration with the "boys" in the band.

Good Neighbours
by Angel Propps

'This rain is never going to stop,' Lisa said sullenly as she stared through the grimy window of the fourth floor apartment. 'We are probably going to need a boat just to get out of here for work in the morning. I mean rain and on a Sunday, could it be any worse?'

Chrissie looked up from her crossword puzzle and bit back a smile at the pout on Lisa's full bottom lip. While she never encouraged bad or bratty behaviour she had to admit it was cute at times and that moment was one of them. 'I'm sure it will slack off and we'll be able to get out and do something, honey, calm down.'

'I hate the rain.' Lisa knew she was whining but she didn't care, she was bored and restless and in the mood for a game, the question was how to entice Chrissie to play. Just when she was considering simply tossing herself across her lover's lap and demanding a good hard spanking followed up by a nice hard fuck there was a loud and urgent knock at the door.

The two women exchanged puzzled looks and Chrissie yelled,' Who is it?'

'It's Marie and Jo, we live next door, we're your new neighbours,' a light thin soprano announced from the hallway. 'We just wanted to say hello.'

Chrissie rolled her eyes and Lisa bit back a grin. They

had seen the moving van but not the neighbours and had been thinking of ways to avoid them. The last neighbours to live in that apartment were nosy, insistent people who were always knocking on the door to borrow things and they were not in the mood for a repeat of that situation.

'Maybe they'll leave if we don't answer,' Lisa said hopefully but Chrissie just laughed and opened the door. The couple standing there were the epitome of butch-femme. The butch was a thick and solid woman with short black hair, moody brown eyes and a mouth that was full and sensuous. Her partner was a tall, elegantly wasted to bone, redhead with porcelain skin and not a single freckle on it. Chrissie could not stop the grin that spread across her face at the sight of them.

'We're really sorry to drop by on you like this,' said the butch in a husky voice that made Chrissie's nipples tighten, 'We don't usually but we had some questions about the tenant rules list that was tacked to our door this morning.'

Lisa began to howl laughter and she said, 'Oh come in, please and don't worry about that list.'

The couple moved inside the apartment and Lisa waved a hand at the book-covered couch, realised it was covered with books and shoved a space clean for the two before adding, 'That's just Nelda down in 4-C. She makes up all kinds of lists and everything else, she drives us all crazy with them. Just run like hell when you see her coming and stand very still and say yes ma'am over and over again when she corners you in the lobby and you'll be fine. She's a bit loose in the head but harmless.'

'I'm Chrissie and that's Lisa, by the way,' Chrissie said as she sat and silently telegraphed Lisa to morph into a hostess, 'Would you like some wine or maybe tea, coffee?'

'I'm Jo,' the butch said and held out one strong solid hand. The instant that flesh made contact with Chrissie's a warm tingle flooded her crotch, 'This is Marie, we'd love some wine.'

Lisa had seen Chrissie's interest and her own was piqued. She and Chrissie were both femmes who loved pretty dresses, frilly underwear and keeping their blonde hair long. Where Chrissie sometimes liked butches to fuck her willing and lushly curved body Lisa preferred femmes that matched her slim height and the one who had just moved in next door most certainly did. She kept sneaking peeks at the four inch stilettos on Marie's slender and pretty feet, at the hem of the cute white dress that kept creeping up those thin flat thighs and she knew Chrissie well enough to know Jo's well tended leather jacket and black jeans had her salivating. She went to the kitchen and took out a bottle of deeply red wine, four glasses and a corkscrew. She put them on a large tray then added small plates of washed seedless grapes, a hunk of soft and delectable Brie, rich wheat crackers and a small array of deli meats sliced so thin they were nearly transparent.

In the living room Chrissie had crept noticeably closer to Jo and Jo had not moved away, in fact she had leaned in. Lisa took that in and the relaxed way Marie leaned against the sofa cushions, watching the two of them with a smile playing along the corners of her mouth and she knew without a doubt that the very boring afternoon was about to get very un-boring.

She poured wine and they all helped themselves to the small meal, chewing slowly, watching each other with hooded and lust filled eyes. Jo absently stroked Marie's upper thigh and Marie leaned very close to Lisa's ear to ask her questions about the neighbourhood in general.

Lisa was a little tipsy but not drunk, she knew Chrissie would punish her for behaving badly so she sipped slowly at her wine, letting it warm her belly while her eyes wandered the expanses of creamy flesh that Marie revealed in her constantly creeping-higher dress. Chrissie watched Jo with the same avarice.

'So is there a ... uh ... perhaps a good kink scene around here?'

At Marie's question Chrissie's eyes sharpened. 'Well, we belong to the local scene,' she said slowly, 'I'm a switch and Lisa is a submissive. We play at the dungeon over on the east side because it's queer friendly and we can swap partners there. Are you two ... monogamous?' She about held her breath after that question left her mouth.

'Not at all,' Jo said calmly and the heat that had been building in the room got hotter, the air shimmered with it. Lisa could feel her pussy growing slippery with desire and she wished Chrissie would just make the move or let her do it. 'Are the two of you?'

'Not at all.'

The silence spun out for a moment and then Marie, her voice filled with mischief, asked, 'so what are you two doing for the rest of the afternoon?'

'You two,' Chrissie replied. 'Now the question is – who gets who?'

'I don't think that's much of a question,' Jo smiled. 'But we have tons of fun toys and no room in our place. Would you be willing to host us?'

'I'll get our toy bag, you go get yours,' Lisa said and leapt to her feet.

Marie was perched in a chair, her legs had been spread over the arms and lashed open so the pink meat of her shaved smooth cunt was exposed. Her wrists had been cuffed and her arms were extended over her head. The black silk rope attached to the cuffs had been pulled through a hook, which held a potted fern in other circumstances. Her tits were forced out and forward, her belly in, and her shoulders were trembling with strain and excitement as Lisa was forced to strip.

'I said take those fucking panties off,' Jo said and Lisa whimpered but she did it, her satiny skin gleaming in the cold light filtering through the blinds. Chrissie knelt on the floor, her clothes long since discarded and her eyes fastened to the sight of Marie's body as it strained against the bondage. To say it was lovely was an understatement. She had sweetly curved hips, a high and perky little ass, long legs and her breasts, while small, were perfectly formed and capped in pink nipples that begged to be sucked.

Jo stood proudly straddle-legged, her dangerously muscular angles drawing the eye to the enormous cock she wore in a black leather harness. Chrissie wanted to simply shove her face on to that cock and suck it till she made Jo come but if there was ever a time to be a good girl this was it. It was rare for her to be able to switch and she always enjoyed it. Right then her pussy was so wet it dripped cold and slick fluids down her inner thighs. She rubbed her legs together, enjoying the sensation, and a moan broke from her throat when Lisa was told to get on her knees in front of Marie.

Jo positioned Lisa first. She put the small raised square of plastic that held a large upright cock between the woman's thighs then shoved her down onto it. Lisa sobbed out a 'yes' as her pussy expanded and took that dick inside and she squeezed her thigh muscles to intensify the pleasure that was already overtaking her.

'Eat her pussy,' Jo ordered, 'And understand this, the way you treat my girl is how I'm going to treat yours. Fuck her good and Chrissie will get fucked good. Make her come and Chrissie will get to come. And so will you. But if you fuck this up nobody comes, do you understand me?'

A bolt of exquisite fear and lust jolted through Lisa at those words. 'Yes, I understand,' she whimpered and bent her face to the glistening wet pussy in front of her. Her tongue lapped at it, opened the labia and licked the soft folds. She took her time, letting her mouth explore every inch of the flesh. She tasted it, licking creamy drops of come that were beading up at the hood away and grunting with satisfaction when more came her way.

Chrissie whimpered and moaned as her mouth was suddenly filled with long inches of thick cock, she gagged and gasped for air but didn't fight, she had long since learned how to survive a good face fucking and she meant to prove it. Jo arched her hips, slamming the cock into her wet and willing mouth. Chrissie gave a long cry of surrender as hard hands tangled into her hair and pulled her closer, as hips bucked into her face and she was forced to open her mouth wider, to take every inch as far and deeply as she could. The need to come built inside her, her tits grew wet and slick with sweat and still Lisa teased and tormented Marie, taking her to the brink of an orgasm as she slowly rode the cock inside her own cunt. Chrissie could not keep her eyes off the sight of that tongue licking that pussy, the sight of flesh meeting flesh making her groan and whimper as she suckled more furiously at the dick between her lips.

'Oh fuck!' Marie sobbed and her back arched out as an orgasm came roaring out of her. Come squirted in gooey white pulses from her pussy, dripped across Lisa's cheeks, ran down her throat and she licked at it with the starved delicacy of a cat, lapping and sucking and catching every drop while Marie strained and begged for more.

'Stop,' Jo ordered and shoved Chrissie to one side. She fell sideways and excitement burst through her, it became amplified when she saw Jo reach for the face dildo, an ingenious little device that was strapped around a hapless wearer's face and held in place by buckles. Jo yanked Lisa's head back and attached the dildo to her face. 'Now we are going to fuck. I am going to fuck Chrissie just as hard and deep and good as you put that cock in that hole in front of you. If you make her come I will make sure you get a reward. But if you don't ...'

Chrissie crawled closer. She needed to see what was happening; Jo took advantage of the situation by positioning herself behind Chrissie, spreading her ass cheeks wide and sliding two fingers into her hot, wet pussy. She was very pleased when those fingers came back out covered in heated oil, she put the fingers in her mouth and sucked on them, savouring the taste of Chrissie's cunt while Lisa began to slowly move her face closer to the dripping hole, positioning herself so she could look over at her lover's face as she began to move that cock in and out of Marie's cunt.

'Tight isn't she?' Jo asked and then she rammed her cock into Chrissie. Chrissie screamed and her hips flailed at the air but Jo would not be pulled in, she gave Chrissie three short and hard slaps on her ass that made her instantly stop moving. 'Fuck her,' Jo said, 'If you want Chrissie to come make her come.'

'Make her come dammit!' Chrissie yelled. Her eyes watched with greed as the cock strapped to Lisa's face drove deeply into the thick lipped pussy that was so helpless against it and she whimpered as an answering thrust was echoed inside her own cunt.

The room was filled with the sounds of fucking. Cries and pleading words banged against the walls as Marie gave into the cock filling her cunt, watching Jo's face closely to see when her orgasm was impending. Lisa was helpless against the orgasm spurting across the cock she was riding. The sensation of being used so harshly, of being made to service another so her lover could get pleasure caused her to fall deeply into sub space and she came again and again as Chrissie grabbed her hair in both hands and viciously slammed her face against Marie's cunt. The sound of cock slapping into pussy was very loud. Jo arched her ass and beat her cock harder into Chrissie, enjoying the sight of pussy opening around that cock, swallowing it and giving it back so reluctantly.

'I want to come!' Chrissie wailed and Jo laughed, 'Tell your girl to make mine come then, make her come good too dammit.'

'Make her come, dammit, Lisa, right now, you make her come!'

Lisa did not need the order, she knew that Chrissie needed to come and she shoved the cock deeper into Marie's come-streaked cunt, then used her fingers to manipulate her swollen and throbbing clit.

Marie felt the orgasm jolting out of her and she began to sob as come leaked and ran down her thighs, pooled into the chair below her and Jo fucked the woman in front of her even faster and harder. She fucked her so hard that Chrissie was being yanked back and forth, her body totally at one with the cock being given to it. Her pussy clenched, opened, clenched and opened. Her mouth opened and a long desperate growl rumbled up as she felt the friction crest into an explosive orgasm that sent her flailing against Jo's wide and sturdy hips while tears rolled down her cheeks and her legs shook with exhaustion. Jo came, her come pouring into the leather of the harness and she fell forward, collapsing onto Chrissie's smooth warm back.

For a long few minutes there was only the sound of heavy breathing and little sighs and whimpers as the last aftershocks of orgasms rippled through their bodies. Eventually they stirred and began sorting out the tangle of arms, legs and cocks. Toys were cleaned and stowed and Jo and Marie found their clothes.

At the door Marie turned to Lisa with an impish grin and said, 'I was afraid we would hate our new neighbours,' and the foursome began to giggle.

'We have to do it again,' Chrissie said and Jo agreed. Chrissie and Lisa stood in their wrecked come-spattered living room surveying the wreckage of a long Sunday afternoon and then Chrissie said, ' Look, it's finally stopped raining.'

Lisa hugged her, enjoying the feel of their skin meeting and melding together. She brushed a kiss across Chrissie's cute little button nose and said,' let's go out, honey.'

'Shower first?'

'Might be a good idea.' Lisa's pretty blue eyes sparkled and her mouth trembled with suppressed laughter.

'The only thing better than having good neighbours is having a good woman who understands you,' Chrissie said, and Lisa nuzzled her neck for a minute then kissed her cheek.

'Nothing better than being understood,' she said, 'I totally agree.'

That Girl!
by Landon Dixon

The flight from LA was long, the drive from Fargo even longer. But, finally, I located the nursing home on a tree-lined street in Merricourt, North Dakota. And then I found "Buffalo" Bob Simmons himself, 102 years old and still frisky as hell.

'I'd like to talk to you about ... "That Girl",' I said, sitting across from the old man in the sunlit recreation room.

His head jerked away from the nurse's aide bent over a fellow resident, his eyes off the woman's large, round buttocks stretching out her tan skirt, and focused on me. 'That Girl!' he murmured, cornflower-blue eyes shining. 'You know, the guys on the team gave me the nickname "Buffalo" Bob, because I came from a hick town in North Dakota, and they all thought buffalos still roamed the Great Plains back in the 20s. But she always called me "Buff". I was her biggest fan.'

I punched on my recorder, poised pen over notepad. 'You're the last surviving member of that 1927 college football team – the "Howlin' Pack", as you were known. And there've always been rumours about the team and "That Girl", star of silent cinema. So, I'm trying to find out once and for all, before it's too late: were the rumours true? Did you and the team and she engage in wild orgies and ...?'

'Fitz called her the hottest jazz baby of them all. And Dot Parker said she didn't have "That", she had "Those" – upstairs and down.'

Bob Simmons' eyes grew misty. 'It was the age of ballyhoo,' he went on. 'America was on the greatest, gaudiest spree in history, nowhere more so than in Tinseltown. And since there were no pro football teams for the Hollywood crowd to follow, they came to our games ...'

'Hey, Bob, is that who I think it is?'

We were on the field, warming up before our second home game in front of 76,000 fans, and I looked towards where our star halfback, "Touchdown" Tommy Lockerton, was pointing. 'Ho-lee!' I gulped, hardly believing my eyes. 'That's-that's Sara Button!'

I'd just seen her in Children of Paradise that summer, and now there she was in-person, the greatest silent film star of them all, standing on the sidelines watching us warm up. Her hourglass figure was poured into a red jumpsuit, her smooth, shapely arms and legs bare, her wild mop of orange-red hair blowing about her heart-shaped face in the warm October breeze, a smile on her bright red Cupid's bow lips.

Tommy elbowed me in the ribs. 'Remember to keep your eyes on your blocks, big guy,' he said, only half-jokingly.

I kept my eyes on my blocks, all right, clearing the way for Tommy to score three touchdowns, all the time knowing that Hollywood's first authentic sex symbol was watching our every move. We easily rolled up our second straight win of the season. But the even bigger thrill came later, when Sara Button bounced into our locker room after the game to congratulate us all.

We were a young, innocent bunch, and a lady in the locker room had us grabbing for towels, to cover up. 'Where've *you* boys been all my life?' she cracked, grinning and smacking her gum, her dark doll's eyes travelling all over us, her apoplectic manager trying to drag her back outside.

'Everyone's invited to my place for a victory party,' she announced. Then she fluttered her long, dark lashes at me, looking directly at my towel. 'No bedroom scene or nothing, you understand. Just food and dance and fun, fun, fun!'

We all crammed into a couple of flivvers and roared out to Sara's house in Beverly Hills, singing our fight song at the top of our lungs all the way there. And what a spread it was – the house and the buffet table! A mansion with huge green lawns and surgically-trimmed shrubs, a teardrop swimming pool in back, the "training tables" inside loaded with all kinds of food and drink and smokes. And at the centre of it all was That Girl, dancing and laughing and flying around with a mad gaiety that perfectly encapsulated the Roaring 20s, her Panatrope record player blaring out Bix Beiderbecke and the King of Jazz.

There were plenty of other good-looking dishes there, too, some famous movie stars, some not. But I couldn't take my eyes off Sara. She had heaping helpings of both T and A, but being a buttman from back in the day when my second grade teacher had bent over to pick up a paper airplane I'd tossed, my eyes were usually glued to her gorgeous glutes. She was just a little thing, maybe 5'2' or so, but her bottom was round and plush and ample, and just about falling out on either side of that tight jumpsuit of hers.

The party went on and on, well past our curfew. But I didn't. I was out like a klieg light after my fourth glass of bathtub gin, woke up in the early dawn on the strangest bed in the strangest room I'd ever been in. I was flat on my back, but I was looking at myself. Because there were mirrors in the canopy of the bed, a giant grinning Buddha squatting on the baseboard, Oriental fans and paintings covering the walls of the room, incense burning somewhere.

I heard giggling, and I turned my bleary eyes to the left. And almost had them pop right out of my head.

Sara Button was lying on the bed next to me, in the arms of another woman! Both babes were naked, and they were kissing each other, passionately and roughly like men kiss women, their pink tongues sliding out and entwining.

I don't know if Sara saw that my eyes were open or not, but she sat up on top of the other woman and arched her back and ran her fingers through her hair. Giving me a nice clear view of her tits, hanging huge and heavy off her small frame, nipples shining red as her mussed-up hair, body blazing white in the early-morning sun.

I swallowed, as quietly as I physically could. I was in Sara's secret Oriental Room – her "loving room", as she called it – watching the other woman's hands travel up Sara's smooth, glowing body and cup her firm, ripe melons, squeeze them. Sara mewled like a kitten, grasping the other woman's hands clutching and kneading her tits, fingering Sara's swollen nipples. Just out of the wheat fields and fallen off the hay truck, I'd never seen anything like it before – two hotsy-totsies making love to one another.

My body and face flushed hot as the Southern California sun, only a dick-length away from the wanton pair. And that's when I finally figured out that I was as buck-naked as the two lovebirds, because I saw that my cock was pitching a silk sheet tent right alongside the sexy ladies. But they didn't seem to take any notice, too preoccupied playing with each other.

Sara spun around and crouched down on the bed, showing off her rear-end to me and the brunette, the sweetest, most hand-pliable, teeth-sinkable pair of seat cushions I'd ever laid on eyes on before. Then she crawled backwards, her brazen buns rippling, until her bum was over top of the brunette's pretty face, knees straddling the girl's head.

The brunette gripped Sara's butt cheeks, sinking her scarlet dragon-lady fingernails into the creamy-white flesh, making Sara murmur and me dry-lick my lips with longing. Then the woman stuck out her tongue, speared it into the ginger bush just below Sara's incredible ass.

That Girl squealed with delight, her rump shivering, the woman licking Sara's pussy, eating out the living doll's snatch. As Sara dipped her head down and her own tongue into the brunette's pussy, licking and sucking. It was the 69 muff formation of every hot-blooded male's fantasy, come true right next to me. My body and cock surged with excitement.

The brunette really knew what she was doing, too, because she had Sara bucking and bleating in only a couple of minutes. The little babe's big buttocks jumped and shuddered, as Sara wildly orgasmed on the end of the other woman's tongue. She kept right on lapping at the brunette's pussy, though, until that bob-haired beauty gasped and shook with her own orgasm.

I could hardly control myself, so wanting to pile-on to all that lovely female flesh. Sara shifted around in her girlfriend's arms again, the two women kissing, licking their sticky juices off one another's faces, their bodies and breasts pressing hotly together. I copped a quick head-turn and stared at the pair, shocked to see that the brunette was also a film maven; Sara called her "Yummy Dearest", and her arched eyebrows, glaring eyes, and plush lips would go on to star in a multitude of sound movies.

And just when I thought the two minxes had fallen asleep in each other's arms, I felt a warm, soft hand slip onto my bare chest under the silk sheet, slide down my tightened stomach and wrap around my wildly beating cock. 'Yowza!' I groaned, closing my eyes and gritting my teeth, the hot little hand swirling up and down the length of my raging prong.

I came almost instantly, spouting hard and often into the sheets, that small, deft hand milking me to sweat and sperm-drenched empty. I heard Sara sigh, and I turned my head, stared into her veiled eyes. Her head was nestled on her girlfriend's tits, and she smiled at me and murmured, 'Touchdown!'

We kept rolling on, winning game after game. And after we'd crushed one of our neighbouring rivals, Sara invited us all back to her Beverly Hills mansion for another party. But Coach was wise to the situation by now, and assigned a couple of freshmen to watch the frat house where we all lived.

So, Sara roared up the street in her big red roadster, horn honking and fiery hair streaming, her red Chow dogs sitting up on the front seat and barking away. It was quite a sight, and the freshies couldn't help staring – as we all snuck out the secret back window in the frat house and met up with Sara a couple of blocks over.

We hit the heights that night. After plenty of good eats and good Canadian whiskey, the guys all got naked and jumped into Sara's swimming pool, still sober enough to marvel at the Persian rug on the bottom of the giant dunk tank. Scantily-clad and unclad starlets jumped in with us, splashing around, nipping at our dicks underwater, getting breast-stroked.

But the star of the follies, as usual, was That Girl. She was energy unlimited, party girl extraordinaire, roller-skating around the edge of the pool in just a flimsy nightgown, daring the guys to catch her. Laughing and teasing, a whiskey bottle in one hand and champagne in the other, a lit cigar in her mouth. Like Fitz said, the ultimate flapper: pretty, impudent, worldly-wise and briefly-clad and hard-berled as possible.

When she got tired of the roller derby, she kicked off the skates and picked up a football. 'C'mon, boys, time for a touch game,' she yelled, racing out on to the lush green lawn beyond the pool, me and Tommy in hot pursuit. The glowing orbs of her rippling butt cheeks in the moonlight were like twin beacons to me, spurring me on to all manners of recklessness.

Sara spiked the ball down in the middle of the lawn and then set up over top of it, in a hiking stance, waggling her bum at us. I elbowed Tommy out of the way and got in behind her, Tommy playing defence. My cock went as hard as a game at Notre Dame, staring at that wagging bottom, then slipping my hands in beneath.

'Oooh!' Sara yelped, my fingers brushing up against her furry pussy. 'You big brute,' she said, turning her head and grinning at me.

I rubbed some more, her fur soft and springy, and damp. She moaned, undulating against my fingers. I got so excited I wanted to grab her by the waist and slam my cock into her pussy – or ass.

But she read my thoughts, and cracked, 'A minute

man, huh? The minute you know a girl, you think you can fuck her!' Then she slammed the football up into my hands and took off.

She ran a hook pattern, big tits bouncing and big buttocks clenching, and I threw the ball to her. She caught it, squeezing it against her chest and turning to run up field. But Tommy right away tackled her, scooping the little vixen up in his arms and holding her squirming and giggling against his chest.

Then, as I watched with hanging jaw and humming dick, Sara dropped the ball and wrapped her legs around Tommy's waist, her arms around his neck, and giddily kissed the guy. He grabbed onto her butt cheeks, and she grabbed onto his cock and jammed it into her pussy, as impulsive and wild as any Hollywood harlot!

Tommy started pumping his hips, fucking the impetuous redhead clinging to him, raining down kisses on his face. I could hardly believe my eyes, watching the pair go at it right out there in the open backyard. And as I quickly glanced around, I spotted another guy taking in the action along with me, from the sidelines, half-hidden in the shrubbery off to my left.

He was the lanky lineman with the hitch in his gait and drawl in his speech that we all called "Pilgrim", and who went on to even bigger movie fame than Sara and her dark-haired girlfriend. He had a broken right hand – which kept him out of the '27 starting line-up – but his left hand was working perfectly fine, fisting his cock, as he watched Sara getting thumped by Tommy.

I turned back to the action, just in time to see Sara drop out of Tommy's arms and scoop up the football, rush over towards me, her mouth open and hair flying and breasts bounding. She was the Galloping Ghost, only a million times prettier. And I ran right into her, blocking her progress.

She collapsed to her knees in a puddle of laughter and beauty, right at my bobbing cock level. She grasped it, stroked it.

'Whoopee!' I groaned, jolted like I'd taken a forearm shiver to the leatherhead.

Sara's swirling hand felt wonderful on my straining hard-on, tugging me even harder and higher. And when she wrapped her ruby-red lips around my knob and sucked on it, I felt like I'd just been sent sailing through the goalposts for a score.

She clutched the base of my cock and bobbed her head back and forth on the shaft, sucking deep and hot and wet, lips sealed tight. Tommy came up behind her, and she dropped down on to her hands on the grass, dragging me down to my knees with her mouth on my cock. Tommy dove back into her pussy, doggy-style, rocking her back and forth on the end of my pole. As I dug my fingers into her thick red hair and helped her out with her sucking, pumping her cauldron of a mouth.

Sara stared up at me with that sultry silent film gaze of hers that had stiffened the dicks and wetted the pussies of a nation of moviegoers, her sensuous mouth full of my pistoning cock, her pussy getting stuffed on the other end. It was too much for me – the wild abandon of it all – and I grunted and went off in her mouth, blasting my joy. Just as Tommy creamed her pussy. And Pilgrim fanned his six-shooter all over the bushes.

We finished the season with a tremendous record, but were shut out from playing in the only Bowl game available. So Sara saw to it that we didn't go unrewarded, throwing her biggest and bawdiest party yet.

It took place at the epicentre of sin-sational Hollywood

decadence, the Garden of Allah Hotel. Sara rented out their largest room, and loaded up one long table with a feast fit for triumphant Roman warriors, another long table with an Al Capone army of bottles. And at the head of the two tables, in between them, reclining on her side on a specially- designed padded platform, was the reigning Whore of Hollywood Babylon, her goddess-like body covered in rose petals.

'Buffet's open, boys!' she cried, when we entered the room.

The Howlin' Pack charged at her, ignoring the laden tables of chow and booze. Carnal appetites were always served first in the City of Angels.

We surrounded Sara, stripping off our duds and giving the silent screen gem an 11 gun salute. She licked her crimson lips, dark eyes gleaming, excited as hell to have the starting team buck-naked and at her beck and call.

'Consider me your trophy,' she breathed, stretching out on the platform and arching her back, thrusting her breasts up and nipples jutting into the air, rose petals sliding off to reveal everything. Then she kicked out a foot, spinning the platform around length-wise. She lay flat on her back and spread her legs, ginger bush glistening a welcome.

Willie "Pepperpot" Sanders was the first to take the plunge, shuffling forward and driving his cock into Sara's waiting pussy. She moaned, stretched like a cat, grabbing on to a couple of other guy's cocks hanging out near her head, and stroking. Chet Forde was directly in line with her face draped over the edge of the platform, and he fed his meat into her open mouth, all eight or so inches of it.

Sara's throat and hands worked, sucking and pumping, Pepperpot pile-driving her pussy. Until he bellowed and blew, made room right away for the next guy. It was the wickedest team huddle any of us had ever been involved in, a gangbang of collegian proportions. Sara writhed around on the platform giving out blowjobs and handjobs galore, getting pussy-stuffed with cock after cock.

Artie "Over the Top" Pickford couldn't control himself, going off in Sara's tugging hand and striping her tits, lathering her body with jizz. A couple of guys quickly grabbed up champagne bottles and emptied them over Paramount's leading lady, washing the hedonistic woman's body with the bubbly while she kept right on smoking cocks like she smoked Gitanes.

It went on and on, wobbly-legged guys going for seconds and thirds, pumping and jerking, the sweat, sperm, and bootleg spirits flying in equal measures. That Girl didn't need a scenario script for this scorching performance, the wanton wench working the crowd to everyone's utter delight, giving the performance of a lifetime.

Until, at last, it was my turn at the gates of heaven, the nexus of sin and debauchery – in between Sara's wide-open legs, in line with her sodden pussy. I'd been holding back, getting stroked and getting sucked, but not taking the ultimate plunge; hoping, maybe, for something special in the end. I was Sara's biggest fan, after all, and her favourite football player of them all.

And sure enough, she looked up from the fringe of dangling, dripping cocks and grinned at me. 'The best for last, Buff,' she said. 'The ol' end-around play.'

She rolled over and reared up onto all-fours, and shook her plump, plush ass at me, pressing a button that lowered the platform down to exactly my cock-level. I doused my dick with champagne, then poured a golden stream of it over Sara's buns, so that it rushed in between her cheeks. She shivered, shuddered her fleshy buttocks at me, and I gripped my goalpost and thrust it in between her luscious mounds. I hit the lady's pink pucker and plowed on through, piling my body up against her behind, buried to the bone.

'Oooh, yes, Buff! Fuck me, Buff! Fuck my bum, will ya!' she wailed, her Brooklynese accent more pronounced the dirtier she got.

I grabbed hold of her narrow waist and moved my hips, sliding my cock back and forth in her gripping chute. The feeling was just this side of paradise, pure bliss fucking that silver screen idol's ass. She received 8,000 fan letters a week; well, here was her biggest fan, giving it to her special delivery.

'Faster, Buff! Faster!' she hissed, always in a rush for her kicks. She shoved her butt back, bouncing her cheeks off my thighs, impaling herself on my stake.

I cranked up the pressure, churning my hips and pounding her bum, her chute a heated, silken tunnel I never wanted to exit. My thighs banged out a frenzied beat on her buttocks, making them dance and shimmy, my cock gone white-hot in her bung, hitting the high notes, ready to trumpet jism into her bowels.

The team stood around in awe, Sara cursing and clawing at the platform, me flinging myself into her bottom, setting her and I and the room to shaking. And then the Big One hit. I buckled and blasted, jetting sizzling semen into her ass in mind and soul-shattering bursts. Sara screamed like the crowds when Lindy landed, frantically rubbing her pussy, her overstuffed ass gyrating on the end of my pumping, spunking cock ...

The big-bootied nurse's aide walked over, wiped "Buffalo" Bob Simmons' chin off. He pinched her juicy bottom a thank-you before she left.

'So,' I rasped, 'the rumours were true, then? About the

college football team and the silent film star – the orgies and the gang-bangs?'

'Sure, they were true,' Bob sighed, folding his hands in his lap and smiling. 'But we had to deny them, for the good of her and our reputations, and careers. But now that I'm the only one left …'

'Did you keep in touch with her after the football season ended?'

'"In touch" is one way of putting it,' he laughed. 'She got me some acting work after I graduated, but I was no ham. The talkies were coming in then, anyway, and Sara developed a bad case of "mike-fright" – it killed her career.'

He looked at me wistfully. 'By 1930 the party was over for Sara Button and the rest of the country. They used to ask her, you know, just what it meant to be That Girl. She'd pout out a frown and say, 'I really don't know. See, I'm just a woikin' goil.' And I'm here to tell you true: boy, could she ever work it.'

Alive
by Clarice Clique

When the end of the world came there wasn't much left we recognised. The landscape was barren, brown nothingness stretched further than the eye could see, towns and cities vanished into rubble, the skies were grey with no sign of birds or insects. What was left was the smell of his sex pushing into mine, the tenderness of his hands on my breasts, the sounds of our soft moans filling the empty air.

We survived because we'd been underground; the two of us on our own personal caving adventure, forcing our bodies into tighter and tighter spaces as if we were journeying backwards into the womb of mother Earth. When we emerged we stared around us, stared at each other and began to cry.

Later when the coldness of the night came we were still standing in the same spot, neither of us having spoken as if when the world had disappeared it'd taken all words with it. The sky darkened into a murky blue-black, if the moon was still out there it was hiding behind thick black clouds, nothing was left but shadows. It was then that we kissed.

Gently at first, our lips barely touching as if we still possessed the shy virgin bodies we had when we first met, but then the thing inside us, the anger, the fear, the hatred, the fear, the grief, the fear, burst free. I bit down on his lower lip until the warm blood flowed between our mouths. He put his hand around my throat and pushed me backwards. The breath struggled to fight its way out of my lungs. I smiled as my head pounded. He smiled back at me and released his grip. We pulled at zips and straps, shedding our clothes like excess skin, baring our flesh to the cold night air in defiance of life itself.

Our bodies were distorted mirrors of each other, pale white skin covering lean hard muscles, he was two inches taller, my hair was blonder and longer, but we felt as if we were the same. The slight curve of my chest, the hard pinkness of my nipples, the neatness of my sex compared with his protrusion, those were the differences, but when we made love I imagined we were one body, neither male nor female, and the way he looked at me at those times made me believe he thought the same.

Now there was nothing feminine about him, he was pumped with testosterone and so was I. We threw ourselves together like beasts. He tugged on my hair, strands ripping out of my scalp and tried to force my head on to his erection, I dug my nails into his balls and nipped the head of his cock. His hands pressed into my flesh pushing me on to my front, I pushed back against him, twisting my body, wrapping my legs around his waist. We bucked and thrust, clawing and biting and bruising the person we loved most in the world. We screamed and we cried our bodies pulsing with orgasmic energy.

When we stopped tremoring we curled up together, his head resting on my chest. I stroked his hair and breathed in his familiar scent. Neither of us slept, we passed the night in the space between dreams and reality not daring to think about what we'd do in the morning.

***

The morning arrived. Earth was continuing to turn on its axis, but there was no beautiful sunrise, the darkness gradually faded into greyness. The only thing that was the same was his early morning erection. Smiling, I shrugged away from his embrace and sat astride him. He opened his eyes and smiled at me riding him, then frowned. With the back of his hand he caressed my battered body and I did the same to his. The contact hurt, but neither of us winced away. We needed the physical pain as much as the gentle caress.

'What happened?' he asked.

I shook my head and pressed my finger against his cut lip. It was too early for some questions.

Later, days later, when we'd made love many times without ever repeating the ferocity of that one occasion, when we'd discovered there was no longer any accessible internet and our mobile phones were useless, when we'd driven as far as our petrol would take us, he asked again.

'What happened?'

And I shook my head again.

At first we talked about nuclear survival and poisoned earth but soon we were drinking from brown puddles and chewing on dead grass. Over time we became experts at scavenging, digging through ruins with bleeding hands until we found the treasures we sought: dried food; tinned food; matches. We chose a van to start with and hoarded our finds greedily in the back, but at some point we got tired of siphoning so much petrol and moved to a smaller vehicle, digging holes for storage points (we had found tools by then so our chafed hands got a rest) and making complex maps. We never saw anyone, living or dead. Then the world changed once more.

He found a radio, together we messed around with it until we got it to work. Neither of us expected anything from it, it was a pointless activity to keep us amused and give us something to think about, like the countless hours we'd spent playing computer games in the time before. When it gave a loud crackle we laughed, when I turned the dial and we heard what could be a human voice, we stared at each other unable to breathe. Our work on the radio took on a new intensity, we swore at ourselves and each other until we found the human voice again and this time we could hear it; a woman in a light Scottish accent repeating again and again the name of a town, pleading with whoever heard this message to come there.

'We have to go there,' he said.

'Why?'

'Because there is nothing else to do.'

We packed as much as we could in the car and set off. As we drove away from the area I thought of as ours, the place that had begun to feel safe, I mentally recited all the prayers I could remember from my Catholic school days.

The car didn't make it. We were forced to abandon it and most of our supplies, taking all that we could carry in over-laden rucksacks and bags.

Hiking more miles than it felt our legs could take before we found another usable car that we managed to start. We held each other but we didn't make love in those times, our bodies warning us that we needed to preserve all our energy. Secretly, I wouldn't have cared, but I couldn't say it to him, "We're going to die, there's no need to prolong it, let's die exhausted from love rather than wait for the madness of hunger or whatever worse things could be waiting for us."

The car didn't make it, but we did.

A community of eight couples waited for us; they greeted

us as if we were their saviours and bombarded us with their names. In their eight voices, with much overlapping, they talked about the miracle of survival, some sort of endurance camping trip in the highest of the Highlands, their plans to make boats and contact other people who made it through, which hadn't come to much so far, but they were so pleased, so very pleased, that we'd responded to their radio message. We were the only ones who had.

'So what's your story?' one of the male voices asked.

We looked at each other, opened our mouths, but we could not speak.

'There's plenty of time for questions,' one of the female voices said.

'What are your names?' someone else asked.

'I'm Daniel and this is Mara,' my lover said.

He took the rucksack off his back and offered them the contents. I was amazed at the quickness of his generosity, to so soon trust these strangers with our world, but I copied him with an attempt at a smile. They received them like manna from heaven but we soon saw our provisions were nothing to them. We were led through their home which was the old ruins of an abbey, and it was a home, there were paintings drawn on the wall, space divided into rooms with carefully placed stones and a kitchen brimming over with stores. Their foraging trips and whole organisation was on a different scale to the scavenging that had kept us alive.

In the evening there was a roaring fire, someone had found and caught a brace of rabbits which were now roasting in its midst. They told us this was what most evenings were like. Everyone, apart from us, told stories and then as the fire burnt out, settled down to sleep not far from the glowing embers. A couple was left on guard duty, Daniel volunteered us to keep watch. I was relieved when his offer was gratefully declined.

A woman came over and gave us a sleeping bag; she squeezed my hand and smiled. 'Don't be scared,' she said. 'We're all safer together.'

Warm wrinkles creased up around her eyes as she spoke. Her and her partner's names, Joy and Rob, were the only ones I remembered. They looked as healthy and as enthusiastic as everyone else, but they stood out for being older, the confidence of their stance as much as the flicker of grey in their hair.

'Thank you,' I said.

'Now get some sleep.' She walked back to Rob and I watched as she bent down to embrace him, blushing when she turned back to me and clearly winked.

Neither Daniel nor I got any sleep on the first night of our arrival. We clung to each other and listened. We'd grown accustomed to silence without realising it and now the air was filled with the sound of our new friends' love making. I tried not to look but sometimes a scream or a moan would make me glance over before my brain could stop me. The couples were not discretely hiding under their blankets or in the darkness of the shadows, their bodies were contorted into all kinds of sexual positions, proud in the remaining light of the fire. Women were going down on men, men were going down on women, their bodies were twined together standing up and lying down, women were bent over in front of their lovers, women were sitting astride their men, grinding for their own pleasure. Joy was in the last category. The practical clothes she'd been wearing earlier were either fully removed, or pulled aside, revealing full heavy breasts that swayed with her movements on top of Rob. She gazed back unashamed when she saw me looking, and it might have been my imagination, but it seemed she ground down harder on her man, rubbing and squeezing her chest for my benefit.

I turned away and pressed my cheek against Daniel's.

'Of all the people that might have survived, we've discovered a sex cult,' I whispered only half joking.

'I know,' he replied, fully serious. 'We've been very lucky since the end.'

We were both aware of the hardness of his erection underneath his trousers, reaching out for me, desperate for release, but neither of us said or did anything else that first night.

The weeks progressed and we became integrated into the community. Everyone was supposed to be equal but it was Joy and Rob who were always asked for advice and looked to for the final decision whenever there was a dispute. Daniel and I did as we were told and answered all their questions about things we'd seen. We learnt to sleep through the noise of the night, although my dreams were disturbed with sexual yearnings for things I didn't know previously existed in any part of my mind. My subconscious haunted me with images of masked people, whips and chains, violence and shouting; in the mornings I awoke covered with sweat barely able to constrain my desire.

We never partook of their nightly ritual and merged our lust with theirs, our opportunities came when we were sent out alone. On hunting-gathering trips we marvelled at the sight of trees and living foliage, watched the rabbits bounding about far longer than anyone else before we killed them, then we quietly undressed and rolled together on the ground. Both of us wanting to feel every drop of dew on the grass, smell every living scent, as much as know each other's bodies.

One day Joy and Rob took us aside, they did all the speaking, talking about the possibility of journeying south and facing the empty landscape we'd described against the risk of staying here and waiting to see if there were still seasons and attempting to survive the bitterness of a northern winter. Then Joy smiled, she leant into me and kissed me on the lips. I felt the full sensual softness of her touch for a moment before she just as quickly pulled away.

'You looked so worried, darling, I thought you'd like a kiss.' She gave Daniel and Rob the full benefit of her smile before she turned her attention back to me. 'Rob and I have been talking and we are concerned that you feel prohibited in your natural behaviour. We want you to feel as relaxed in our little community as everyone else does. There's really no reason that you shouldn't be.'

'Joy's talking about sex,' Rob said with a wide smile to match his partner's.

I looked him full in the face and was struck by his movie star good looks that I'd been struck with many times before. I knew I was blushing and was grateful when Daniel stammered out a reply to them.

'We both feel very relaxed and part of the community. We're both very happy. We're comfortable'

'There's no need for you to sneak off to have a bit of fun,' Joy interrupted him.

'Unless that is what you truly want and then obviously no one cares in the least, but we're worried that it's because you feel too shy to join in,' Rob said.

'You're such a quiet little pair,' Joy said. 'But you can see that everything of our old lives have been swept away, including all the societal and sexual prohibitions that once guided us. With everything that has happened I think we can permit ourselves and each other the freedom to take pleasure and enjoyment where we can.'

'But,' I said. All three pairs of eyes gazed at me yet there was no more I could say, just "but".

'If you are willing Rob and I can help guide you on your journey.'

'What journey?' I asked.

Your journey of sexual discovery,' Rob said.

'Well, you two think about it, and if you're interested we're here for you tonight, or any other night.' Joy squeezed my hand, flashed her smile at us and then she and Rob walked off holding hands to check on how the stores rationing was progressing.

Daniel and I glanced at each other.

He spoke first. 'They're right, the world has changed and maybe we should change with it.'

'We have a fire to make.' I walked off and after the smallest pause he followed me.

That night as the fire began to die down I looked over to where Joy and Rob were sitting. Rob winked at me, I responded by blushing and staring down at my feet.

'We should go and talk to them,' Daniel said. 'I think it'll be good for us.'

'I don't know.'

'Neither do I. I just think that maybe, maybe we should see where it leads us.'

'And if it's a bad place?'

'We get in the car, drive somewhere new and be together just the two of us again.'

I nodded, unable to process all the emotions competing inside me.

Joy and Rob showed no surprise as we walked over to them, I felt conspicuous, sure that the others were all looking and knowing and laughing. But it wasn't like that, in the evening whatever struggles had marred the day were forgotten and all of them were full of love for themselves and everyone else. If any of them noticed us they would have smiled and been happy we were committing even further to this life. I told myself this as we stood awkwardly in front of Joy and Rob's smiling faces.

Rob stood up, took Daniel's hand in his and led him back to the place that Daniel and I slept together every night. I looked back at Joy, unsure what to expect, unsure how I'd imagined Joy and David freeing us from our inhibitions. There was no time to form my thoughts. Joy's hands were on my jeans, expertly undoing them and pulling them down my legs. I did not move.

'Don't be nervous. A little bit of fear now and then can add to the excitement, but never be nervous.' She slid my knickers down to rest around my ankles with my jeans.

The night breeze swirled around me, exploring the new nakedness of my lower body. I shivered. Joy wrapped her body around me as if she was trying to cuddle me into warmth.

'Have you been with many different people?' she asked.

'Only Daniel.'

She smiled up at me. 'Then believe me there's a very special pleasure in tasting something that is not yours.'

Her head pressed between my thighs, her tongue, warm and wet, darting out and immediately finding my secret spot. She licked and lapped at me.

I moaned softly at first and then louder as my body turned into a mass of nerve endings all seeking pleasure. I looked down at Joy, at the strange beauty of having this woman touch me. I forced myself not to look over at

Daniel and Rob but I couldn't stop myself picturing the charismatic older man on his knees with my lover's cock in my mouth and it hurt my heart at the same time as the ecstasy flowing from Joy's tongue exploded through my body.

She laid me down on her rug and held me against her breasts, my cares disappearing amidst their soft warmth. I listened to the beat of her heart.

'I've very sensitive nipples. Kiss them. Dream that they are covered with some wonderful food, something you'll probably never taste again in real life.'

I thought of cream, peaches, strawberries, their fresh sweetness, and then I obeyed her and took her nipple into my mouth. I kept my eyes closed and sucked. The food disappeared from my mind, all I needed to think about was what I was actually doing, lying in the arms of another woman, immersed in her ample bosom as she stroked my hair. I kissed one nipple then the other, caressing the one that didn't have my oral attention. Joy arched her back into me and moaned loudly. I cradled the weight of her breasts with my right arm, marvelling at their firm softness in the same way that Daniel and I looked at the grass and the rabbits, amazed that something beautiful still existed in this world.

'Would you let Daniel see your body? I don't know if that is the right thing to ask. Forgive me if it isn't.'

She squeezed me tightly against her flesh. 'It is the right thing to ask, but for tonight, be selfish, just think of your own desires, things you've always wanted but have been too shy to talk to Daniel about.'

I took a deep breath. 'I think I'd like you to spank me.'

It seemed a strange thing to request, even as I said it, while I was bathing in the warmth and comfort of her body. But then everything in this new world was strange.

I kneeled down in front of Joy, the palm of her hand thwacked against my bare skin. It sounded loud to me, cutting through all the other sounds, but in reality the other couples were in their own worlds more or less oblivious to what Joy and I were doing. Apart from one couple. Daniel would be imagining me just as I couldn't help picturing him, even as Joy told me not to think of him, to be selfish and concentrate on my own pleasure. As her hand continued to thwack against my skin my eyes raised and I looked through the smoke from the fire to where Daniel was on his knees, his head raised, staring back at me. Rob was behind him, his rough hands on my lover's hips, thrusting in and out of him. I felt every thrust as if it was my tightness being pushed into. Later I would kiss and caress all the places Rob touched him, later he would kiss and caress all the places where Joy touched me, but right now we gazed into each other's eyes, our heart beating fast from the pain and excitement of sharing our love.

Joy spanked me until my skin was raw, then she kissed my buttocks and pushed a finger in between them. I gasped, she pushed deeper into me.

'Do you like that?' she asked.

'Yes, I do, don't stop.'

'I think you can take more.'

Another finger pushed into me, or maybe it was two fingers, I felt stretched as if it was a man behind me pushing his sex into me. I pushed back against her, she leant over me, the weight of her breasts on my back as her fingers fucked my ass. The pleasure made my body shake, the night air filled with my screams. Joy grabbed a handful of my hair and pulled my head back to kiss her.

'I'm not finished with you yet,' she said and went back to finger fucking me even harder than before.

I orgasmed twice more under her touch before she let me rest. I moved to walk back to where Daniel and I slept but Joy held me tightly in her arms.

'You're mine tonight.'

I nodded and laid my head on her breast, falling instantly into a deep dreamless sleep.

Something changed between Daniel and I after that night. I don't know if it was a good something or a bad something, things were just different. When Rob or Joy wanted sex with one of us we obediently trotted over. The weeks passed and we began swapping with the other couples until there was no one in the community that one of us hadn't had sex with. The weather started to get colder but the talk of moving south disappeared.

Then on one of the days when the wind was blowing extra bitterly Daniel kissed me and told me he wanted to move on.

'Why?'

'I want it to be the two of us again. I want to be lonely together.'

I nodded, understanding without understanding.

They tried to talk us out of it, they cried as they watched us packing, but gave us more and more supplies until we couldn't fit them into the car. I don't know if they carried on crying when we drove off, I didn't look back and neither did Daniel.

We live hand to mouth, mouth to hand. Daniel says he's happier, he only wants me. Sometimes I say it was easier in the group, but mostly I kneel in front of him sucking his cock.

Yesterday he asked me if I wanted him to spank me.

'It wouldn't be the same,' I said.

He nodded and we made love facing each other our

limbs entwined.

'We're doing well, aren't we?' he said.

'Yes, we are,' I said squeezing my sex around his. 'We're still alive.'

The Couple with the Dragon Tattoo
by Giselle Renarde

It was always a giddy thrill, those nights we met up with Vijee and Lilliana. For people like Gerry and I, so deeply entrenched in our boring little heterosexual lives, having dinner with a lesbian couple was exciting. Maybe it shouldn't have been, but it was. The fact that Lilliana and Vijee actually identify as polyamorous pansexual BDSM enthusiasts was just the icing on the restaurant cake.

Prior to Friday, there had never been any suggestion something sexual might happen between the four of us, but that possibility always hung heavy on the air. We knew about their lifestyle, though not from them directly. Friends at our *Introduction to Printmaking* course had pointed out Vijee and Lilliana, and told us all about the girls' "lifestyle". They warned us to "steer clear of those freaky dykes", to be exact. So what do you think Ger and I did the next week in class? Why, we pulled our chairs up to Vijee and Lilliana's table, of course.

Ever since, the four of us have held a standing bi-weekly date for Friday nights. It baffled me that the pair would want to waste their precious time together with a boring couple like us. In fact, I still feel a little honoured every time Vijee e-mails me to confirm dinner. I like them both. So does Gerry. They're fascinating people in their own rights, and together – well, we've never known anyone like them!

Vijee and Lilliana are a long-term committed couple, much like Gerry and I, but they don't live together as we do. Vijee is mother of three, and married to a man who knows all about her relationship with Lilliana. For ages I wanted to ask if her husband ever "joined in the fun", but I could never work up the nerve and I wasn't sure if it would be rude. Gerry isn't quite as concerned about coming off as a louse – or a letch, for that matter – so on Friday night he asked the question for me.

'No,' Vijee said in response. 'This relationship is just for us.'

Lilliana smiled at her and they clasped hands at the table, squeezing so hard their knuckles turned white. Seeing those two together, it was hard for me to imagine Vijee with a family, with a husband. It was harder still to imagine Lilliana's home situation. She acted as submissive to a married couple, a man and woman, and she lived with them in a house she described as "absolutely brill". Rather than paying rent or contributing to household expenses, she cooked and cleaned for them. She cared for the minutia high-earning business people hadn't time for. In exchange, they provided her free room and board as well as a moderate salary and, as Lilliana put it, "certain pleasures you might not understand."

True, Gerry and I had never been BDSM people, but that didn't mean we weren't curious. We've tied each other up on occasion, but according to Vijee and Lilliana, that's child's play. I wondered what they got up to in the bedroom, I really did. I'm sure Gerry and I would have been terrified at the sight of it. Terrified... and tempted...

'Oh, big news!' Lilliana announced. 'We finished our dragon tattoo!'

'Dragon tattoo?' When I shifted closer to Gerry, he put his arm around my shoulder. We'd neglected to make reservations, and the best our restaurant could do was cram the four of us at a circular table near the bar. Knees brushed knees. The setting was intimate, to say the least.

'You both got dragon tattoos?' Gerry asked.

'We both got *a* dragon tattoo,' Vijee said.

I was reasonably confused, but Gerry beat me to the punch. 'How do the two of you share a tattoo? One gets it Monday to Wednesday, the other Thursday to Sunday?'

Lilliana burst with a genuine giggle. Vijee tittered along, but her laughter was more subdued and obviously insincere. Sometimes I wondered if Vijee disliked my boyfriend, but it was hard to know. She was gruff with everyone.

'It's one tattoo,' Lilliana explained, 'but it's on both of us.'

'So it's the same tattoo and both of you have it?' I asked. This conversation seemed more confusing than it ought to be.

Vijee put her arm around Lilliana's shoulder. 'It's one design, one grand scheme, one concept. It's a double-headed dragon wrapping itself around both our bodies.'

My insides tingled at Vijee's pronunciation of *bodies*. That word became flesh in my mind. I couldn't help but picture she and Lilliana naked together, kissing, writhing, their skin etched with multicoloured dyes. Dragon heads raging. Dragon tongues mingling. Dragon eyes glowing. I felt my face flush as somebody's knee brushed mine. My heart raced against the cage of my ribs.

Gerry must have been thinking what I was thinking, because he kissed my hair so slowly I felt the heat of his lips on my scalp. When Vijee did the same to Lilliana, I nearly laughed. Our dinners always seemed to turn into these couple-versus-couple public-display-of-affection competitions. Gerry and I were not the lovey-dovey type. Generally speaking, we didn't do much more than hold hands outside of the house. There was just something about this pair, about the freedom of their hands and their lips, that either put us at ease or stimulated our competitive natures – I'm not sure which.

A childlike grin leapt to Lilliana's cheeks. Her eyes sprung wide before settling into mischievous slits. 'Hey, do you want to see it?' She looked to Vijee as if to seek permission, and when Vijee nodded she asked again. 'Want to see our tattoo?'

Gerry was perched so near to me I actually felt him gulp. 'You want to show it to us?'

I smiled. I couldn't help myself. Looking around for our absentee waiter, I said, 'Why don't we pay for the drinks and then head back to our place? We can pick up some take-away en route. Doesn't look like our server's the least bit interested in taking our orders, anyway.'

The invitation felt forward as it spilled past my lips, but I couldn't seem to contain it. I would never have asked them out of the blue, but in light of Lilliana's offer ... well, I felt I had to jump on it before they changed their minds.

Vijee insisted on paying, which was not uncommon. Most weeks Gerry argued with her, but I think he was every bit as anxious as I was to get our friends home and out of their clothes. Even before we'd settled up, he was coaxing me into my jacket.

'Shaggy,' Lilliana cooed as he fidgeted in his chair. They called him Shaggy as a tease, because Gerry reminded them of the lanky character from Scooby-Doo. At least, that's why they claimed they called him Shaggy. 'He is a bit of a dish, isn't he?'

My breath held fast to my lungs as I looked up at Vijee, but her expression betrayed no trace of jealousy. It never did during Lilliana's mild flirtations. Was Lilliana talking to me, then? Was she asking if I thought my own boyfriend was dishy? 'Well, yes,' I finally said. 'Of course he is.'

'You hesitated,' Gerry teased, nudging me in the ribs. I could hear the smile in his voice as I observed the twinkle in Lilliana's eye. 'You don't think I'm dishy at all!'

'I do,' I shot back. I was beginning to feel flustered now, by the impending weight of the evening's play. It was exactly what we'd hoped for, what we'd discussed at length, what we wanted…but in a sense, there's nothing worse than getting what one wants.

We left the restaurant, deciding to forego take-away. I couldn't have eaten a bite anyway, not with the conflation of anticipation and doom flitting through my core. My pulse raced as we walked home from the restaurant. Gerry and I rushed on ahead, arm in arm, while Lilliana in her five-inch heels and Vijee, who was less than a pillar of physical fitness, struggled to keep up.

I was all excitement when I reached for my keys. They rattled in my hand as I brought them to the door. Gerry had to hold the damn things steady as we slid the metal key into the lock. We turned it together.

Our flat hardly seemed our own when Vijee and Lilliana filtered in. There was something foreign about the space. It smelled fresher than usual. Perhaps that was only Lilliana's bright citrus perfume I was catching on the air as we all took off our jackets and tossed them on the sofa. Everything felt new, streamlined and ideal. The flat seemed cleaner than usual, despite the sink full of dishes and the plates of half-eaten biscuits Gerry managed to spread about the place. None of that mattered.

I caught Gerry's eye, and felt overwhelmed by the love glowing there. When he reached for my hand, I gave it to him without hesitation. 'So, then,' he said, weaving his fingers together with mine. 'Let's see this dragon tattoo.'

Lilliana nodded to the bare front window. 'Somewhere a little more ... private?'

Vijee looked her up and down and cracked a smile – a rarity. It wasn't that Vijee was mean or irritable; she just wasn't one for smiling. Every time she grinned or chuckled, it felt like a great reward. I found myself seeking her approval, hoping she'd grant me so much as a smirk, and when she did I always felt strangely elated.

'The bedroom,' I said, almost in a whisper. The word had been stuck in my throat. 'Come into our bedroom.'

'This is a lovely flat,' Lilliana said as I led the way.

Gerry went on about the neighbourhood, proximity to the trains, and assorted nonsense, but his familiar voice soothed an ache in me that could only be described as insecurity. There were things we'd always wanted, Ger and I, and I was chuffed to bits we'd experience them together. What's a long-term live-in boyfriend for if you can't share him with a polyamorous couple?

Lilliana and Vijee leaned against our bed as Gerry confessed to stealing a wireless internet signal from the people downstairs. I pressed my cheek to his shoulder, hoping he'd never stop talking. I needed to hear his voice. He chattered on even as Lilliana unbuttoned her ruffled black shirt and slipped off her velvet shirt. Leaning back against the wardrobe, I felt I was watching a film of two women undressing in my bedroom. It all seemed surreal.

Vijee disrobed as if by magic. One moment she was fully clothed, the next she stood at Lilliana's side in nothing more than a black bra and knickers. Lilliana struggled out of her lace-trimmed satin slip, but it got stuck at her large breasts and she needed Vijee to tear the bloody thing over her head. 'What would you do without me, heh?'

'I'd keep my clothes on, I reckon.'

Gerry rambled on about refitting the fixtures, but I think everyone had stopped listening to him by that point. Certainly, I had.

'Are you ready for the full effect?' Vijee asked.

'Absolutely!' I clapped my hands in front of my chest, transported back to my sister's hen night – male strippers and all that. Lilliana and Vijee's bodies were far less firm, and yet this was wildly more arousing.

Vijee unfastened her bra at the back, letting it fall forward as she pushed her black panties to the floor. It wasn't until Lilliana kicked off her big boots that I realised for the first time she and Vijee were the same height. It was also in that moment I got the full effect of the wild colours streaked across their skin. *There be dragons!* With that mirrored tattoo caressing Lilliana's porcelain skin and Vijee's darker flesh, they reminded me of the yin yang symbol. A green, blue, and purple dragon wrapped its thick, serpentine body around their legs and bellies. One head swept past Lilliana's left breast, the other head past Vijee's right breast. The girls wrapped their arms around each other's waists and both dragons kissed tongue to tongue, like the snakes of the Caduceus.

When Vijee turned slowly to Lilliana and licked her just behind the ear, I heard Gerry inhale sharply at my side. My pussy pulsed as I watched them, and my hand sought Ger's, fluttering like a blind bird. His fingers clasped mine as we gazed lasciviously at the real-life movie playing before our eyes. Vijee cupped Lilliana's pixie face in her hands and ran her tongue all the way up the girl's face, from her chin, past her painted lips and her nose, all the way up to her forehead. I couldn't help wondering if it was an act of care or ownership, like a mother cat licking her kitten. *I love this and it's mine.*

'I can take pictures, if you like,' Gerry blurted. They both looked to us without separating head from head. 'Of the tattoos! Sorry, I meant ... nothing sleazy. Photos of your tattoos, and the two of you together. I've taken courses. I'm not terrible at it. We can borrow a white screen from my mate and we'll do like a pro shoot.'

'Not tonight, I hope.' Vijee brushed her fingers through her black bush. 'I'd prefer to do some hair removal before we immortalize our ink.'

'Me too,' Lilliana said, though her pussy was nearly bare as it was. She had only a slight strip of dark hair above the V of her thighs, which looked faintly like an arrow pointing down.

Gerry shook his head. 'Not tonight. Another night. Skip our next dinner, maybe? Do it on a Friday?'

'Or Tuesday after Printmaking?' I suggested. I wanted them to know I was on board with this, with all of it ... whatever *it* was.

Nodding cheek to cheek with Lilliana, Vijee let a sly smile bleed across her lips. 'Go over there.' She slapped her girl on the behind. 'Go tell Shaggy thank you.'

Lilliana brought her hands up to her cheeks so her forearms blocked our view of her hard cherry nipples. She stood in front of Gerry like a shy child compelled to thank her uncle for a Christmas gift. Dropping her hands to her sides, she pried my fingers from his and raised them to her bright red lips. She held Gerry's fingers so close to her mouth I was sure he could feel her breath on his skin. I found myself experiencing Gerry's desire, anticipating her next move.

'Thank you, Shaggy.' It was little more than a breath

but I felt her words inside me, coaxing juice from my lower lips.

Just when I thought Lilliana would kiss my boyfriend's knuckles, she extended his index finger and slowly closed her mouth around it. Ger let out a glorious groan that pulsed inside my core. She sucked on his fingers one at a time, consuming, letting each one in until her lips touched his knuckle. It was mesmerizing and magnificent to watch her sucking those fingers like five little cocks, devoting care and attention to one and all. She was a minx, that girl. My excitement at having her in our bedroom was surpassed only by the control in Vijee's eyes as she looked on.

'And thank you, too,' Vijee said to me. She leaned against the bed and patted the mattress. 'Come, Marva, sit. This stands to become an extended *thank you*.'

Lilliana nodded in eager acquiescence, her mauve-grey eyes on me all the while. My pussy throbbed as I watched, speechless. I could have sworn my feet never touched the ground as I cut a quick path to the bed. My body felt weightless next to Vijee. In fact, I nearly tumbled into her lap when I sat down beside her.

We watched in silence as Lilliana unbuttoned Gerry's shirt, sucking his fingers all the while. The sound of his belt unbuckling and his trousers unzipping summoned the sweetest of aches between my legs, and I was certain Vijee recognized my distress. I watched her watching me in the mirrored wardrobe. Vijee and I were so much darker than Lilliana and Gerry, and I wasn't sure what that meant, if it meant anything at all.

'Does this make you at all jealous?' Vijee asked as we watched Lilliana pumping Ger's erection in her smallish hand. 'My girlfriend jerking off your dear Shaggy – are you envious at all?'

'Envious? Yes. I love touching my boyfriend's cock. But jealous? No.' I breathed a sigh like fresh summer air. 'No, I'm not jealous at all.'

And that was God's honest truth. Watching them together was like watching true-to-life porn, a film created exclusively for our enjoyment. It nearly killed me to resist touching myself as he and she pressed their naked bodies together. Vijee must have felt the vibes, because she set a hand on my thigh and whispered, 'Will he be jealous when I do the same to you?'

I didn't speak. I couldn't. As much as I'd expected this, I wasn't sure what to do when the moment arrived. Her hand moved the length of my thigh, warming my flesh as it travelled. Vijee's soft brown skin was lighter than mine, but her fingernails were painted the same pink as the pinstripe shot through my grey slacks. I felt too "business" in the outfit I'd worn tonight. If she undressed me, perhaps I'd be more comfortable?

'Shall I suck it, Shaggy?'

I looked up to find Lilliana on her knees in front of my Gerry. Her back was done up too, though her long dark hair concealed much of the dragon streaking across it. The blue, green, and purple monster crossed one cheek and the other thigh before wrapping around her calf.

Meeting my boyfriend's beseeching gaze, I nodded until he nodded too. 'Yes,' I mouthed.

'Yes,' Gerry said, looking down into Lilliana's face. His hard cock rested on her lips. She seemed so worshipful there between his legs. 'Please do.'

My chest filled with warmth as I watched Lilliana's mouth open to receive him. Pressing him back against the mirrored door, she plunged her face against his pelvis. A pleasured moan rippled from her throat, echoing through my Ger.

'Oh, Shaggy!' she cooed, her speech garbled by his cock. 'You're getting huge in my mouth.'

Gerry and I released an undulating breath together, though we were half a room apart. It was in that moment, as Lilliana sucked my boyfriend's cock and Vijee's stroking closed in on the heat between my legs, that I fully understood the dragon tattoo. I understood how it could be one thing shared by two people. I understood how Lilliana could live with her Master and Mistress and Vijee could live with her husband and children, and yet this couple was always together. Desire flooded my veins. I wanted to *be* that dragon. I wanted to be that force of love that enveloped those two and stayed with them even when they were apart.

That's when I kissed her.

Vijee seemed stunned when I let her up for air. She obviously hadn't expected me to pounce. She didn't anticipate I would press her shoulders down against the mattress and straddle her, fully clothed. I knew she was used to being in control. With Lilliana, she was the boss in the bedroom. With me? Well, she'd just had to take it as it came.

I tore off my top and tossed it on the floor. The bra went too. 'Take off my slacks!' I said with all the urgency beating in my body. I slid my back down on the mattress, letting my legs hang off the side while Vijee scrambled out from under me. Our quick fingers touched and tapped as we struggled to get me out of my clothes. When I was naked, she jumped on me and kissed my mouth. Though thoroughly winded, I kissed her as well, feeling the sides of her warm breasts as they pressed against mine. I could hear Lilliana sucking and slurping at my boyfriend's cock. Those sloppy wet noises combined with Vijee's as she descended my body to lick my pert nipples.

The dark pink of Vijee's tongue looked so gorgeous against the dark brown of my tits that the image sent a wave of electric heat straight to my clit. I didn't want her to stop. My pussy was gagging for it and I couldn't deny her the pleasure.

'Lick me!' I cried, pressing rudely on Vijee's head. 'Please, oh please, I need it!'

'Lick her!' I heard from behind Vijee's shoulder. It was Gerry, of course, encouraging Vijee as I'd encouraged Lilliana. My belly felt warm at the sound of his voice, and I raised the soles of my feet up to the mattress and pressed harder on Vijee's head. When she snaked off the bed and I noticed Gerry and Lilliana behind her, I smiled so widely I thought my cheeks would break.

'My lover,' I whispered. I didn't know what else to say, but it didn't matter. He knew.

When Vijee's tongue met the juicy folds of my pussy, I just about died. Gerry went down on me every so often, but I always suspected it would be different with a woman. It was. She didn't attack me like he did, in aggressive stabs and strikes. Vijee licked me slowly and sensually with her mouth's pink velvet. Up and down her strides seduced me while Lilliana moved with force, back and forth, on Gerry.

Nothing in the world had ever felt this good, or made me feel so marvellously alive. Once she'd warmed me up, Vijee wrapped her arms around my ass and went at my clit hard and fast. She knew what she was doing, this one. She knew to caress and then strike. She licked my clit so deliberately and in such quick repetitions that I nearly lost my mind. My eyes shut tight as I forced my crotch against her face and locked her there with my thighs. Perhaps it was overkill to hold her head against my pussy with my hands, but I did that too.

I bucked my hips, pushing my bush against her face, not caring if she felt uncomfortable or even humiliated. I suspected, from the cries she issued as she sucked my clit, that she was enjoying this every bit as much as I was. Thrusting myself against her face, I screamed through orgasm after orgasm. *Our poor neighbours!* I reached for a pillow and pressed it to my face to keep the volume down.

How long did we spend gripped in that wicked embrace? I came again and again, begging Vijee to stop, but this is where she exerted her force. She held my thighs and sent me over the edge a million times – at least, it felt that way.

'He's going to come!' Lilliana cried so loudly I heard her through the pillow covering my head.

Suddenly, Vijee was gone, giving me the reprieve I'd begged for. My clit was so sensitive I thought I'd die if it so much as brushed a feather. I tossed the suffocating pillow off my head and looked up to see Gerry standing erect in more ways than one. He was much closer to the bed than he'd previously been, and Lilliana was crouched beneath him, jerking him off while she sucked his balls.

Vijee traced her fingernails the length of my thigh, which tickled me in my state of sensation overload. 'Make Shaggy come on his woman,' Vijee instructed. 'Make him shoot cream all over those lovely wet pussy lips.'

I watched in amazement as Lilliana's hand flew against Gerry's hard cock. I didn't know how she could have aimed in that position, but when Ger tossed his head back and howled, his come flew across the room to land hot against my bush. As Ger's warm cream kissed my throbbing pussy lips, Vijee squeezed my nipples and I burst with yet another fine orgasm.

Vijee and Lilliana didn't stay long after that. They probably wanted some "alone time" together – I imagine they never got as much as they'd like. I wondered where they went together if they both lived with other people. How did they secure time alone? Hotels? I wondered, but I didn't ask.

Their departure was a bit of a haze to me. I remember them planning a photo shoot with Ger as the dragon disappeared behind layers of clothing. It was so like a dream. I couldn't quite believe any of it had actually happened. We'd gone to bed with pansexual polyamorous BDSM enthusiasts, and they were set to return so my boyfriend could take photographs of their dragon tattoo. In two weeks' time, Vijee and Lilliana would be naked in our flat again. I was counting down the seconds.

Intrigued
by Sommer Marsden

There are specific rules to things like this. So we figured that out right away. My Daniel had lusted after Dana for ages. Andrew and I had a thing if you counted sexual tension you could cut with a plastic picnic knife. But none of us ever acted on it. We were friends, after all. And why would you fuck up a good thing?

When you're a married couple, it's hard to find another couple you really resonate with. Where everyone gets along, and no one irritates anyone else.

Daniel and I had found that magical couple in Andrew and Dana McCleary. But then there were the sparks, sparks that went beyond things in common and playing cards with a bottle of wine on a Friday night.

I had noticed it immediately. The way my husband sort of blushed when Dana McCleary walked in. The way he poured on the charm when we played Poker. The way he learned to make her rum and cola just so. And I also noticed Andrew's eyes on me. How he always filled my wine when he filled his. How he touched my hand when handing me the paper for charades. How he touched my lower back when he held the door for me at our latest restaurant and I walked past.

So it was one drunken fall night around a fire pit in the backyard that Dana, of all people, brought it up.

'So what would you think if we traded off for a night?' she'd said as if she were offering to share a particularly coveted recipe.

'I ... um ... what?' I was never good at being straight forward and blunt, so I simply lost all words the moment she said it.

'Andrew has a little thing for you, Eileen. I mean you have the long dark hair and the big green eyes and the gams.' Her eyes shot to my legs and her husband chuckled softly.

I felt myself blush a little in the darkness. 'Thanks?'

Daniel's hand had crept high on my thigh as we listened. I could tell by the way he squeezed ever so gently that this talk – whether it went anywhere or not – excited him.

'And I have noticed a certain handsome Daniel Gunn eyeing me up from time to time.'

I snorted and then covered my face. 'Understatement.'

Maybe it was the wine or our long term friendship, but for whatever reason I wasn't angry or offended or even scared. I was intrigued.

'And how would we go about this?' I asked. I reached for the wine but Andrew snagged it and motioned for me to hold my glass up. I couldn't see the hazel of his eyes in the firelight, but his whole face was lit with a devilish glow and when he smiled at me my stomach flexed and my pussy went wet.

What would it be like to fuck him, I wondered. And how would I feel if I knew that while I was with him, my husband was fucking pretty, trim, red-headed Dana?

'We think it would be good to go to something that has a break in it, like an intermission or a pause midway. We go in with our respective spouses, then we switch at the halfway point. At the end, we return to normal. Does that make sense?'

I nodded. 'You know they're playing that Scottish war movie at the Ambassador. They have an intermission,' I said. 'But that would mean either a dash to a hotel or …' I swallowed hard but my cunt flexed and my heartbeat revved. 'Sex at the theatre.'

'There's my girl,' Daniel said softly.

Andrew leaned in and smiled. 'We're game if you are.'

Turned out I was.

I was practically vibrating as the movie wound down to the intermission. Not to mention the fact that all four of us had seen this movie before. It wasn't even new material to keep us occupied. I glanced down the row and doubted a single one of us was paying a lick off attention to the plot.

The lights came up from off to a dim butter yellow glow. *INTERMISSION* rolled across the black screen in white letters. Daniel touched my hand once, kissed my hair, whispered, 'Be safe, I love you.'

And then he took Dana's hand and off they went, leaving me, a bit jittery with handsome Andrew.

'You OK?' he asked, putting an arm around me as we walked out. There were balconies that were shut off to patrons. They were under minor construction and cordoned off with velvet ropes. Very retro, very chic. The Ambassador was an old theatre and the ropes only added to the old-school magic of the building. 'We don't have to do this.'

'But I want to do this,' I whispered as we moved through the crowd. 'I want to do this.'

'Good,' he said right up against my cheek. 'Because I've wanted to do this since the first time I laid eyes on you.'

It all spiralled through my mind then. I would have a

first again. A first kiss, a first touch, a first stroke of outer nether lips, a first flick of my clit with foreign fingers. That first moment when I was entered by a man new to me, wielding a never before seen, touched, or sucked by yours truly cock. All new for me. I shivered as I let him guide me.

'Are you cold?'

I turned to Andrew, his warm hazel eyes kind and hungry and intelligent. 'Nope. I'm excited.'

We tiptoed up the thickly carpeted steps like teenagers. I tried to imagine Daniel with Dana. I expected anger and jealousy and maybe a bit of petulance. But when I really thought of it, as we climbed up the steep steps into forbidden rooms marked off by velvet ropes, I grew more excited. More aroused.

Andrew propelled me into a room with a good bit of roughness and my heart thrilled at it. He pushed me to the wall, shoving my skirt high with one hand and pinning my arms above my head with the other. Daniel and I saw eye to eye almost. Andrew was a good head taller than me. Overpowering me would be no problem.

I tried to breathe and found I couldn't. Wetness slid from my pussy and pooled in my panties.

It wasn't long before he was working the sides of those panties with his big fingers, tugging. He stopped to kiss me, gently and then needy and then hard and I took every single nuance of that kiss, moving my body up into his hands.

'Last chance to back out.' He waited, his cock hard against my leg, his breath tearing in and out of him – a gentleman in wolf's clothing.

'No. No backing out,' I gasped, moving my hand to the hump of his cock and stroking him. His lids lowered just a touch and his breath hitched. A surge of feminine power shot through me and I gave him a little squeeze.

Somewhere in a different upper room someone moaned. Was it Dana? Was Daniel fucking her by now? My stomach tumbled with nerves and I whispered, 'Hurry.'

'Are you in a rush?'

'We have a timeline but it's more …' I shook my head and moved to kiss him.

Andrew squeezed my wrists and I felt the tiny bones grind and a burst of protest from my arms. The pulse of pain added to the intense pleasure of being off with him in this cluttered and forbidden place.

'Tell me, now, little Eileen. Confess.' He pinched my nipples through my blouse and they stood up hard and true.

My pussy flexed around nothing and I wished so hard for a hard cock to fill that void.

'It's more I need it. Soon,' I admitted, my face blazing with blush that neither of us could see. 'Like now.'

And that was really all it took. That confession in a dark and dusty room. He worked his zipper and I shucked my skirt. For a moment there all that we heard was the rustle and hushed chatter of clothing as we took off the ones we could and moved the ones we couldn't.

He kissed me – my lips, my face, my throat. His tongue and teeth worked over my clavicle, then lower to take my nipple into his mouth and biting me so I felt a fresh slide of fluid.

'Andrew, hurry,' I begged him. My blouse and my bra hung open to give him access, my tops filleted whereas my skirt was abandoned in a heap at my feet.

'Put your leg up,' he said and I did. He gripped it to his waist and worked the condom wrapper. I took it from him, rolled the rubber on his long, hard cock taking in the details. A bit thinner than Daniel but longer for sure. Curved to the left instead of the right. Silken skin that flared to a velvety helmet of a tip. I hummed low in my throat and Andrew laughed softly.

'Put me in you, Eileen.'

So I did. I pressed the tip of him to the soaking wet split of my pussy, braced myself for his entry. He gripped my leg to him and my waist in the other hand and drove into me. There was that moment – that magical moment of firsts – where we froze. He was seated deep, all of my body seeming to pulse around his cock, and we just stayed there – still. Locked gazes, breath quiet but fierce and then I pushed my body up to take him in and the spell was broken. Andrew started to move, his mouth clamping down on mine, swallowing my cries as my body inched me close to a release already.

I felt the thick carpeting beneath my feet, an intricate Oriental pattern. I smelled old dust and plaster and heard the general soft din of many voices down below in the old fashioned lobby where other people were not fucking, but eating popcorn and drinking soda. The gentle slap-slap-slap of our bodies meeting filled my ears and somewhere in another room, again the sound of a female moan. Dana.

Andrew growled against my throat at the sound of his wife getting pleasure. My pussy clamped up tight around him and I felt the first spasms of orgasm work through my nerve endings. But he was coming, I could tell by the grip of his hand on my leg and the other on my hip. The thrill of his loss of control wasn't lost on me. I love the sound of a man pushed over the edge. Even if it means I don't get mine, so to speak.

But Andrew had no intention of letting that happen. He pulled free of me, putting his hands around my throat and kissing me hard. The feel of his grip over my pulse made me wonder if we ever did this again – would he hold my neck a bit tighter? If I asked him to?

'I'm sorry for that. I've never fucked you, you felt too good and the noise of them ... got in my head. I tipped too fast.'

'It's fine I ...'

But he wasn't hearing me because he dropped to his knees and knocked my legs apart with his big hands. I realised again that he was so much bigger than me, something I wasn't used to.

His mouth was hot and his tongue was as talented at eating pussy as kissing. 'You taste sweet. Like sugar and peach syrup,' he murmured against the inside of my thigh, nibbling that tissue-paper-thin skin and making all of my flesh erupt in goose bumps.

He raised his arms and found my nipples with his fingertips, squeezing so hard I gasped but then he sucked my clit rhythmically and the pleasure and pain blended into something perfect and indescribable.

I imagined it again, his hand around my throat as he pinched my nipples hard enough that tiny spots of white light blossomed in my vision. Andrew alternated licking me softly with his broadly flattened tongue and sucking my clit hard enough to keep me off balance.

I gripped handfuls of his brown hair and tugged as I came. Losing my manners, thrusting my sex to his face. But he finished me off perfectly and then licked me clean, holding my knees with his hands as if he knew I felt like they would buckle.

Music sounded in the theatre proper. Intermission was ending.

Andrew looked up at me grinning. 'Did I do right by you, Eileen?'

'Good God, yes,' I laughed, offering my hand.

He took it, stood and kissed me – once passionately, once sweetly on the forehead. 'We should get back.'

'We should,' I said and followed him out into the dusty hall. No sign of Daniel and Dana and I wondered if they had fit as well as Andrea and I had.

Daniel put his arm around me as the theatre went black again.

'You good, girly?'

'Very. You?'

'It was nice. But I sure am glad to have my girl back next to me.'

'Admit it, you loved it.'

'I loved it, but I love you more than anything,' he said.

That was all I really needed to hear.

Daniel kissed me and I knew that I smelled like fucking, because he did. Instead of making me anxious or jealous, it made me want to fuck him. Soon.

Dana leaned over and whispered, 'Hey, there's a play running downtown for the next week or so. It's pretty long so they break it up into two hour bits with a forty-five minute intermission. We could meet there and then after go out to dinner. Are you guys interested?'

In the dark Daniel's hand stroked my breast and I felt my body hum to life. Both to get him alone later and to go to this play, to take another opportunity with our new found lovers.

I leaned forward, catching the light gleaming in Andrew's eyes. Again I imagined those hands – so much bigger than mine, so much bigger than Daniel's – around my throat. He smiled at me and I felt my stomach dip with excitement. I laughed softly as the movie started to roll. 'I admit, Dana, I'm intrigued.'

Daniel whispered in my ear, 'That's my girl.'

Quay Party
by Courtney James

Jacqui always had to go one better than me. To say we were best friends, she spent as much time competing with me as she did shopping for shoes or sharing girly confidences over a glass of Pinot Grigio. Whenever I found myself down on my knees, scrubbing away the ring round my bathtub, I was aware Jacqui employed a cleaner to perform exactly the same boring chore. We both owned the same model BMW, but hers, naturally, was a convertible. And she never, but never failed to inform me of the size of her latest pay rise or performance-related bonus. So when I started dating Ray, who was not only a recently retired professional footballer with the physique and sexual stamina to prove it but also owned a beautiful holiday cottage on an isolated stretch of the Brittany coast, I knew Jacqui couldn't possibly top that.

I was wrong.

'Of course,' she told me, as we relaxed in the chill-out area of our favourite day spa, after an extensive top-to-toe pampering session, 'the best thing about Gareth isn't that he has a half-share in the most exclusive restaurant in Newquay.'

'Really?' I said, my heart sinking as I wondered how she was going to better my achievements again.

'No, darling, though trust me when I tell you that not

only is the seafood out of this world, but you and I have a standing invitation to dine at the chef's table.' Jacqui smiled as she sipped her fresh melon and kiwi juice. 'No, the best thing about Gareth is that he owns a boat.'

'A boat?' I raised a freshly threaded eyebrow. 'What, like a model yacht? A rowing boat?'

'Don't be silly, darling. A *boat* boat. He's always sailing to France or the Channel Islands for the weekend. In fact, he's taking me away this weekend. Well, actually, he's taking *us* away.'

'Us?'

'Me, you – Ray, too, if you want to bring him. Oh, do say yes, Mia, it'll be such fun.'

And that's how I found myself in the back of a taxi with Ray, heading through the busy streets of Newquay on a warm Friday evening, about to spend a weekend on a boat with my oldest friend and a man I'd never met before. We'd already had plans of our own, which I'd been reluctant to cancel. Since I'd been with Ray, I'd discovered a taste for role playing games I'd never known I possessed. We mostly enjoyed scenarios where he was in charge. He'd been the stern headmaster to my naughty schoolgirl, forced to spank me for not getting my homework in on time. On another occasion, he'd improvised a toga from my best tablecloth, and we'd played Caesar and the wilful slave girl. Tonight, we'd intended to check into a hotel in Brighton under false names, and give everyone the impression he was my boss and he'd taken me away behind his wife's back. It would have been such fun, but I knew from past experience that what Jacqui wanted, Jacqui usually got. And what she wanted more than anything was to show off her brand-new boyfriend and his big, shiny boat.

The taxi pulled to a halt on the quayside. 'Here you

go,' the driver announced.

'So which boat are we looking for, exactly?' Ray asked, as our bags were retrieved from the boot.

Glancing round, I spotted it immediately. 'There.' The *Lusty Lady*, sleek and silver-grey and moored just to our left, with Jacqui waving from its deck, wearing a little black dress that showed off a goodly expanse of her long, tanned legs.

'She's pretty impressive.' Ray's tone of voice left me wondering whether he was referring to the boat or my friend.

'Hey, come on board and we can get this party started!' Jacqui called down to us.

Exchanging "what the hell have we let ourselves in for?" glances, Ray and I climbed the narrow wooden gangplank. Barely were we over the boat's threshold – if boats had thresholds, my lack of nautical terminology suddenly becoming glaringly apparent – when Jacqui descended from the deck to enfold us both in hugs.

'Mia, darling. So lovely to see you. And you must be Ray ...'

She held on to him for rather longer than is usually acceptable in these circumstances, pressing her long, lean body against his. I'd have been struck with an unwanted pang of jealousy if I hadn't caught sight of the man standing in the far doorway, watching.

The only area where I'd truly believed Jacqui had never managed to top me was with her choice of men, but her latest boyfriend came as close as she ever would. Dark and lithe where Ray was blond and broadly muscular, Gareth had the self-assured stance of a man who'd worked hard for the good things in life and knew he deserved them. His gaze met mine, and in that moment I knew something was destined to happen between us.

When Jacqui at last entangled herself from Ray – and was it purely my imagination that placed a visible bulge in the crotch of his faded denims as they broke apart? – Gareth came over to be formally introduced.

'So you're Mia?' His voice was deep and lilting, forged in the Welsh Valleys. Very sexy. Jacqui really had done well for herself. 'Lovely to meet you. And Ray, mate ...' He clapped Ray on the shoulder. I could swear the level of testosterone rose as the two men sized each other up, like two stud bulls vying for dominance.

'This is such a beautiful boat,' I said, accepting a glass of champagne from Jacqui. 'So where are we going to be sailing to, Gareth?'

'Tonight, nowhere,' he replied. 'Jacqui's cooking dinner, and there's more champagne on ice, so I thought we could all take it easy, get to know each other better. But tomorrow, if the wind's set fair, I thought we could take a little trip to Jersey. Either of you ever been there?'

We shook our heads. It sounded like a good plan. Party tonight, sleep it off in the sunshine tomorrow. Ray seemed to approve, too, making himself comfortable on a leather banquette running the length of the cabin and pulling me on to his lap. Sitting chatting to Gareth while Jacqui bustled round in the small galley, taking something from the stove that smelled rich and savoury, I felt Ray's fingers burrow under the hem of my vest top to trace seductive, spidery patterns on the flesh of my back. My disappointment about being deprived of our planned dirty weekend in Brighton melted away under Ray's subtle caresses. I was sure tonight would end with us having sex in our cabin. We'd have to be quiet, so as not to alert Jacqui and Gareth to our behaviour, something I always found difficult, my natural urges being to scream and sob when I came. Maybe Ray would have to silence me by gagging me with a pair of my own panties ...

Lost in increasingly rude fantasies about what I'd let Ray do to me when he got me alone, I was dragged back to the present by Jacqui announcing that dinner was ready.

'It's funny, Gareth, but I somehow expected you'd be doing the cooking,' I said as I took my place at table. 'Seeing as how you're involved with a restaurant and all.'

'Well, I'm only the financial backer,' he replied, pouring me a glass of Cabernet Sauvignon. 'I leave the actual food preparation to people with real skill, like my lovely Jacqui.'

'Oh, you ...' Jacqui dropped a kiss on his lips, a kiss that grew increasingly intimate, as though they'd both forgotten they had company. Maybe I wouldn't have to worry about disturbing them later; they looked like they'd be cooking up a storm of their own before too much longer.

At last, Jacqui recovered herself enough to dish up the meal. Ray wasn't joking about her culinary abilities; her insatiable desire to be the best at everything had led her to spend a week on holiday in Ireland, studying at one of the country's top cookery schools. The results were evident in the delicious coq au vin she served up, accompanied by creamy mashed potatoes and green beans with slivered almonds

As we ate, we discussed everything from the highs and lows of Ray's football career to Jacqui's forthcoming business trip to Madrid to the famous faces who'd eaten at Gareth's restaurant. For four people who'd never spent an evening together before, we were getting on incredibly well. Though no one said anything, I was certain we were all aware of a discernible sexual vibe around the table. Jacqui and Gareth appeared to be completely into each other, but from time to time I would look up from my plate and see Gareth watching me, the expression on his face one of undisguised desire. His obvious interest sent a pleasurable shiver through me, but he was my best friend's man, and completely off-limits, in the same way I'd expect Jacqui to restrain herself if Ray appeared to be coming on to her.

'That was fantastic,' Ray said at length, setting his knife and fork down on his empty plate. 'What's for dessert?'

'Oh, nothing fancy. I thought we'd have cheese and grapes,' Jacqui replied. 'I went to the nice little deli in town earlier and got some of the fabulous local blue cheese they sell. Tell me, Ray, have you ever had Cornish Yarg?'

'Is that a cheese, or some kind of infection?' he quipped, blue eyes twinkling. At that moment, I thought I could quite easily forget about food altogether, and just let Ray take me down to our cabin so he could fuck my brains out. Gareth, however, had other ideas.

'Jacqui darling, you've worked so hard already tonight.' He patted her on the back of the hand, encouraging her to stay in her seat. 'I'll fetch the cheese, and make some coffee. Mia, would you mind coming and giving me a hand?'

'Sure.' I rose to my feet, helping Gareth collect the dinner plates and take them through to the galley. While I stacked them in the sink, intending to leave them to soak in hot, soapy water, Gareth was busy arranging the cheese and fruit on a wooden platter – or so I thought. Engrossed in what I was doing, I didn't hear him come up behind me at first. When his big, warm hands closed round my breasts through my top, I tried to pull away, hissing, 'Gareth, what do you think you're doing?'

'Shhh,' he murmured, thumbs skimming my nipples. I hadn't worn a bra beneath the skimpy top, and the taut buds sprung to life under his caress. 'I've wanted to do this since the moment I met you.'

'What if Ray or Jacqui see us?'

'They won't. I made sure the door was shut.'

That wasn't the answer I'd been looking for. Gareth had contrived a ruse to get me alone with him, and now he was intent on seducing me, kissing softly along the length of my neck while his hands continued to tease my nipples. His body pressed closer to mine, and I felt the solid length of his cock, nudging against my bum cheek. Already turned on by my fantasies of wild sex with Ray once we'd all retired for the night, having Gareth's big hard-on poking so insistently at me was only causing the heat to rise further.

'You are gorgeous, you know that...' As Gareth spoke, he pushed the hem of my top up towards my neck, so his fingers could clamp around my bare tits.

Almost without thinking, I reached behind me to stroke his dick through his chinos with my soapy hands.

'Hey, you're getting me wet!' he exclaimed.

'You're having the same effect on me,' I responded. The come-on was way too blatant, given I was supposed to be indignant about the fact Gareth was intent on stripping and playing with me, while our respective partners sat on the other side of the galley door, oblivious to events. But it was true; my panties were soaked, clinging to my pussy lips in an annoying fashion. I'd be so much more comfortable if I stepped out of them. So I did.

If Gareth was surprised how quickly I'd dropped any objections to his unexpected seduction, he didn't say a word. He watched with amusement as I kicked my wet underwear under the galley counter, out of the way, turned round and put my lips to his. We kissed as though it was going out of fashion, lost in frantic exploration of the other's mouth with our tongues, tasting red wine and garlic and not caring. This was wrong, we both knew it, but that didn't stop it feeling right.

Part of me almost wished Ray would come to see what was taking us so long, bursting through the door to discover me in Gareth's arms, half-naked and wanton. The way the scene played out in my mind, he wouldn't be jealous, wouldn't fire angry accusations at me and storm off the boat. Instead, he'd join in, peeling down my skirt so I was completely bare, before unleashing his hard cock and slipping it into the cleft between my legs, while Gareth's mouth moved lower, to take one nipple between his soft, sucking lips …

With hasty fingers, I unfastened Gareth's chinos. When he stepped out of them, I saw he hadn't bothered with underpants. His thick, slightly curved cock rose up unimpeded, inviting me to touch. I did, hearing the breath catch in his throat.

I might have come in here to help organise dessert, but now there was only one thing I wanted in my mouth. Crouching down, feeling my knees make contact with the cool, tiled galley floor, I fed the tip of Gareth's cock between my lips. He tasted of earth and ocean both, the rich salt tang of his crotch encouraging me to snuffle deep. His fingers grasped the ponytail I'd fashioned my hair into, so it wouldn't get blown on deck. It seemed only Gareth was getting blown tonight, and he was loving it, subtly controlling the bobbing movements of my head as he gripped my hair tighter.

Mouth stretched widely around the thickness of him, I responded by sucking strongly, using every trick I knew to coax the spunk from his balls. He didn't want to come in my mouth, though. With a little reluctance, he freed himself from the clutch of my throat, smiling down at me as he took a pace back. I knew the make-up I'd applied so carefully would be smeared all over my face, but it didn't matter. The lust etched across Gareth's face told me just how beautiful he found me at that moment.

He picked up his discarded chinos, hunting his wallet out of his back pocket. I could have predicted that was where he kept his condoms; Ray stashed them in exactly the same place. Rolling one into place, he returned to me, slipping a couple of fingers between my legs as he kissed me to check I was ready for him.

'Before I fuck you,' he told me, 'there's something I have to do.' As he spoke, he reached for the door handle. I rushed to stop him. The galley door was the only thing preventing Ray and Jacqui from finding out what we were doing. But as Gareth let it swing open, I saw why no one had come to find out why we were taking so long to make a simple pot of coffee.

Jacqui lay on the leather banquette, her dress hiked up almost to her waist. Kneeling on the floor beside her, wearing only his tight-fitting black briefs, was Ray, his head bent into the fork of her crotch. I couldn't see quite what my boyfriend was doing, but from his position, and Jacqui's little squeaks and murmurs of pleasure, I reckoned he must be using his tongue and at least one finger to stimulate her pussy.

Gareth grinned. I must have looked as shocked as I felt. Had this all been some kind of set-up? Had he and Jacqui deliberately set out to lure us into a game of swapping when they'd issued the invitation to spend the weekend with them, or had events simply followed a course impossible to ignore once the sexual chemistry between the four of us became so evident? I didn't know and I didn't care. Watching Ray lap at my best friend's cunt, I was hornier than I'd been all evening, and nothing was going to stop me being fucked.

Bending over the table, sticking out my rump in invitation, I felt Gareth come up close behind me. In that position, he'd be able to thrust into me while still having a good view of proceedings in the main cabin. As his big, condom-clad cock slid up my channel, I couldn't help letting out a groan. Alerted by the sound, Ray broke off in mid-lick. Our eyes met. I saw no guilt there, only enjoyment. He must have seen the same in mine, because neither of us made any move to stop what we were doing. With a wink that told me to have just as good a time as he clearly was, Ray resumed his oral exploration of Jacqui's sex.

That was all the encouragement I needed to tell Gareth, 'Fuck me.' He didn't need to be asked twice. Long, hard thrusts of his cock had me whimpering in pleasure. He pulled out almost all the way, my pussy lips clinging tight as though they couldn't bear to lose contact with his wonderful tool, before plunging back in to the root. I clung on to the table, buffeted against it with every stroke like a boat on a stormy sea, the friction as my pelvis rubbed on the smooth wood stimulating me in all the nicest places. Gareth's expert fucking was taking me very rapidly to a place where the waves of orgasm would engulf me.

Somewhere in the distance, Jacqui called out, repeating the word, "Yes," over and over, followed by a long-drawn-out cry that could only mean Ray's tricky tongue-work had brought her to her peak. The last thing I saw, before my cunt convulsed around Gareth's cock and he responded with a body-shaking orgasm of his own, was

Ray stripping out of his underwear, cock rearing up proud, ready to give Jacqui the same thorough fucking Gareth had just given me.

The *Lusty Lady* never made it out of port that weekend. When the four of us finally woke the following morning, having pleasured each other almost until the sun came up, we decided sailing all the way to Jersey – indeed, sailing anywhere at all – was a waste of our valuable fucking time. We might have explored most of the combinations we could think of the night before, but there were still a few more to try before we were satisfied.

Jacqui might believe she'd come out on top again, I thought as we breakfasted on pastries and coffee, but when Ray and I invited her and Gareth over to our place, it would be a different matter. Her boyfriend might be gorgeous, and he might have a big, beautiful boat, but mine had a well-stocked toy box and a very kinky imagination, and I knew I wouldn't swap either of those things for the world.

Like a Moth to a Flame
by Elizabeth Black

Amelia emerged from her hot shower. Her skin shone, warm and rosy. The scent of peppermint shampoo and cassis bath gel wafted in the steam that flowed out of the bathroom door.

She had already eaten for the evening. She'd found a drunken Goth who had stumbled out of a club, and she'd overtaken him in an alley. She hated Goths. They were an insult to her kind. His blood wasn't the best she had ever had. He must have been *A negative*. *A negative* blood tended to have a sharp sour quality to it. Maybe it was the cheap booze he drank that made his blood taste so vile. Even though he was not particularly appetizing, she'd needed to eat. She never hunted a new lover on an empty stomach. An empty stomach led to bad decisions. She'd picked a few losers in her past when she hunted on an empty stomach.

She had taken extra care in brushing her teeth. She used whitening strips for two weeks to make sure her teeth were as white as marble. Drinking blood had a tendency to stain her teeth yellow. She grumbled at the waste of 50 dollars, but she knew she could not make a stupefying entrance at the art gallery tonight with teeth that made her look like a chain smoker.

She cranked up Delerium's *"Chimera"*, which played

on her MP3 player. Her entire body felt charged with excitement.

Tonight was the night she would claim Peter for herself, once and for all.

Peter had been her painting instructor for the past six months. She had chosen him for her new lover within the first two classes. She needed a new lover. Her old one had been with her for over a hundred years, but he had deteriorated and had needed to be hidden in her cellar with all the others a few weeks ago. He was useless to her now. She needed a new lover.

Within one week she was sipping red wine at Peter's home, when his wife was busy working at the Celestial Gallery of Fine Arts. Within two weeks, they were naked on the couch in his living room, surrounded by his paintings. His paintings witnessed their frantic lovemaking.

Amelia knew Peter couldn't resist her. She became more enticing to him as the weeks went on.

Amelia had slowly worked her magic on him, introducing him gradually to red meat. He was a vegetarian, but she knew that wouldn't last long in her presence. She soon had him drinking more than the one glass of red wine he drank during the day. She introduced him to Benedictine. She had to prime him for when he would fully become her lover.

Amelia sat naked on her bed. She squeezed some cassis body lotion into her hand, and rubbed it against her freshly shaven legs. She imagined Peter's hands massaging that lotion against her hot skin, behind her knees, against her thighs, and into her hot labia. Her pussy melted at the thought of Peter's touch. She would have him tonight. She was going to make sure of that.

There was one other she would have tonight, and that

was her secret. Peter did not know about it. She'd told no one. Her second lover was to be her treat to herself.

Her new bra, garter belt, and stockings lay on the bed. All were shades of ruby and crimson. Amelia put them on, slowly, one after the other, and imagined Peter standing with her, dressing her. His large but delicate hands gently stroked her skin as he fastened the bra straps. Those hands from which came the most beautiful oil seascapes and nudes of lovely women would mould her skin and press against her hot flesh until she melted in his grip. The silk fabric of the garter belt chilled her skin. The stockings felt as airy as spider's webs as they slid over her legs. Peter liked her calves. She had a dancer's legs. He loved to run his palms over the length of her legs, from her ankles, up her calves, along her thighs, until he reached her heat. Then he pressed his fingers against her and inside her until she was satisfied.

She looked in the mirror. She liked what she saw. She knew Peter would like what he saw too when he tore off her clothing tonight after the art show.

She pulled her new dress from its hanger in the closet. It was a blood red, satin, vintage 1951 sheath dress. The entire bodice and long sleeves were made of Italian lace. The satin felt cool as water as it slid over her body. It hugged every curve. Peter liked to see her in clothing that fitted her like a glove. This dress was a second skin.

Amelia did not want Peter to pick her up. She wanted to make her grand entrance at the Celestial Gallery Of Fine Arts when a crowd of art-lovers gathered in the lobby. Amelia commanded such attention she knew that every head in that gallery would turn towards her as she walked down the steps. Peter's wife was showcasing his artwork this week, along with the sculptures, landscapes and portraits created by other artists in their club. Amelia laughed at the idea of a club. That was so pedestrian. Like a high school popularity contest. Amelia had seen the truly great artists and their works: *Picasso; Rembrandt; Rossetti; Moriseau; Cassatt.* She had taken a few of them as lovers over the years. This "club" to which Peter belonged was juvenile compared to real artists. Peter was above them. He had real talent. Amelia would make sure his talent became well-known, once she made him her own.

Amelia slipped on her three-inch velvet crimson pumps, grabbed her clutch purse and keys, and walked out the door. As she drove to the gallery, she plugged her iPod into her car's entertainment system, and turned on Delerium. She liked to listen to Delerium when she was in an especially wicked mood.

She looked forward to seeing Peter's face when he saw her in that tight red dress. She also relished the thought of his wife's livid reaction upon seeing Amelia invade her gallery space. Amelia never referred to Peter's wife by her name. That would bring her too emotionally close. She was always "Peter's wife" or "the woman". If things worked out well tonight, she would call her by her first name. Amelia had plans for his wife tonight. She would slowly torture her until she could no longer stand it. Amelia knew his wife was fascinated with her. She had seen her drive by her home several times, and park her Lexus on the street, spying on her. Once, in a fit of bravery, his wife had come to her house – to talk. Amelia played her like she played all people who felt threatened by her. She invited her into her home. She served tea and Madeleines. Amelia made it quite clear, as quietly and as calmly as possible, that she would not stop seeing Peter. If Peter wanted to stop seeing her, it was up to him to do that. Amelia knew the problem in their marriage didn't fall on his wife. It was solely Peter's doing. If his wife wanted to confront someone, it should be Peter.

Amelia used the time to learn more about his wife. She was also a painter. Amelia had seen her paintings. Peter had turned her towards painting landscapes, but Amelia thought her depictions of classic myths were better. His wife was surprised to receive a compliment from her husband's mistress. His wife also liked Madeleines, but she had never found the recipe or the tray anywhere. Amelia had an extra tray handy. She gave the extra tray to his wife, along with a recipe to make the delicious little French tea cakes.

His wife did not know what to make of Amelia.

She excused herself to use the bathroom. She had entered Amelia's bedroom quietly. She thought Amelia did not know she had sneaked into her bedroom, but Amelia knew. She watched from a hidden space in the hallway. His wife went through Amelia's clothes, taking out a blouse here and a dress there to sniff them. She opened a jewellery box, and ran her fingers over Amelia's strands of amber and carnelian. His wife immersed herself in Amelia, and Amelia was pleased.

Amelia was familiar with the feeling coming from yet another rival. His wife felt revulsion and attraction at once. Amelia knew how to handle that.

Her thoughts were still on Peter's wife when she parked her car in the gallery's parking lot. Amelia was ready. Tonight she was to put on a stellar performance.

She walked up the stairs to the gallery's entrance, and then opened the door. She waited at the top of the stairs leading into the gallery until a head turned in her direction. Then, another head. Two young, attractive men did a double-take when they saw her. A woman sipping champagne stopped in mid-sentence when she saw

Amelia standing alone at the top of the stairs.

A young, attractive man dressed in a tuxedo walked up the stairs to greet her. He was one of the artists, a sculptor. His name was Jeremy. He offered to show Amelia around, but she declined his invitation, gently, with a cool palm pressed lightly against his cheek. She heard his heart hitch at her touch. Her hearing was very sensitive. She smelled his blood. It smelled spicy and rich. She wanted him, but she could not take him in this kind of crowd.

She told him she was looking for Peter. Jeremy wrapped an arm around her waist, and looked into the crowd. He pointed out Peter standing in a crowd near a painting of a grove and a bridge. Amelia saw him, and her entire body tingled.

There was no sign of his wife. Amelia would deal with his wife in due time.

Amelia stared at Peter, willing him to look her way. He did. She immediately turned to Jeremy, and asked him about his works. Jeremy was pleased to have Amelia's attention. He told her he lived in the area, and he had been a sculptor for ten years. This was his third local show. He had been showcased in Italy and France. He gave her his card with the address to his studio. He scribbled his home phone number on the back, telling her he was not always at his studio number. She should feel free to call him at home. He looked directly into her eyes when he said that.

She knew it was a good thing she had eaten that Goth earlier. She was very tempted to take Jeremy right there on the gallery steps. She was full enough to keep her wits about her. She stifled a belch, and thanked him for giving her his phone number.

She did not see Peter when he stood at her side. She hadn't looked for him. She didn't need to. She knew he would soon appear when he saw her talking to someone as sexy and as handsome as Jeremy. She was right.

'I see Jeremy didn't waste any time talking to you. He gravitates towards the most beautiful woman in the room,' Peter said.

'You know her, Peter? Who is she?' Jeremy said as he stared at Amelia's breasts. 'She's lovely. Have you been hiding her from me?'

'Yes, he has, Jeremy. This is the first gallery show I've been to in over a year,' Amelia said.

'We are being rude, Jeremy, taking up all her time but not offering her a drink,' Peter said. He turned towards Amelia. 'Would you like a drink? Champagne?'

'Yes, I would,' Amelia said. 'Would you like to join us, Jeremy?'

'I would love to.'

They walked to the refreshment table. Heads turned as Amelia walked through the crowd. Some of the women's heads turned towards Peter and Jeremy, but it was clear to Amelia that Peter's and Jeremy's attention was completely on her. She saw men and women gaze at her with longing, envy, and trepidation. She was both enticing and threatening to many men and women in the room. If only they knew how much she could please them.

Peter handed Amelia a flute of champagne. A crowd slowly gathered around them. She basked in the attention, especially coming from Peter and Jeremy.

Suddenly, a voice boomed through the room.

'What the hell is *she* doing here?'

At the sound of Peter's wife's voice, the crowd dissipated. Amelia stared at her, not moving, much the way a snake stares down a mouse shortly before devouring it. Jeremy slid one arm around Amelia's waist as if to protect her. Peter ran after his wife, who strutted about the room in a rage.

'I can't believe you brought her here! This is the opening of my new gallery, and you've *ruined* it!'

'She came on her own. I didn't bring her here.'

'But you knew she was coming! How *could* you?'

'She just wants to see the paintings and the sculpture.'

'I *bet* she does.' His wife ran into the back room, followed by Peter. Within seconds, the gallery went dark.

'I'm sorry,' his wife announced as she entered the gallery lobby. 'The gallery is closing early. Thank you for coming.'

At that point, Amelia knew it was time for her to act. As people left the gallery, she walked to the back room to find Peter's wife. She found her cowering in a storage room, fighting off tears. Amelia walked in, and locked the door.

'Get out!' Peter's wife said when she saw Amelia. 'You don't belong here.'

'I came to see the paintings.' Amelia said.

'And Peter.'

'And *you*.'

Peter's wife stared at her, confused.

'What do you mean you came here to see me?'

'I meant what I said,' Amelia said as she walked towards Peter's wife. The woman looked like a mouse, cowering on the floor with her mascara smeared beneath her eyes. Amelia was so close she could smell the red wine on her breath and hear the woman's heart thumping hard against her rib cage. She was evidently both terrified and thrilled. That was what Amelia wanted.

Amelia placed her hands against the woman's shoulders, and coaxed her to stand. At her touch, the woman shivered. Amelia knew she had her exactly where she wanted her. The craving she felt for this woman was finally about to be quenched.

'I know you're fascinated with me,' Amelia said. Her hands slid slowly around the small waist and her breath hitched at her touch. 'I know you watch my house from your car. I know you've gone through my clothes, my perfumes, my jewellery. You can't stop thinking about me. And I can't stop thinking about you.'

Their lips brushed and the woman stared at her with wide-open eyes. Her entire body shook, but she did not push Amelia away.

'Don't fight it. It's easier that way,' Amelia whispered. She kissed his wife full on the lips. The woman melted in her arms. Amelia's tongue slid into her mouth, and she tasted red wine.

'I've wanted you since I first met Peter,' Amelia said. She kissed his wife on her eyelids, down the bridge of her nose, and against her jaw line. 'Peter is a very talented artist, but he doesn't have your energy or lust for life. I want his artistic spirit, and I want your vibrancy. I want both of you. I know you are fascinated with me. Now, you can have me. Just let go. Don't fight it.'

Amelia pulled a silk scarf away from the woman's neck, and then sank her teeth into her throat. She found the pulse quickly, and sucked gently.

She pressed her hand against the woman's left breast. Her heart fluttered quickly, bouncing against the palm of her hand. As Amelia sucked, she fondled the woman's breast. Her nipple grew hard. Amelia pinched her nipple between her thumb and forefinger. The woman groaned. 'Don't stop,' she whispered. 'That feels good. Suck harder.'

Amelia was surprised. Most of her lovers did not like to be sucked too hard the first time. The suction felt very uncomfortable for some of her lovers. They felt as if they were being suffocated. She was gentle the first time, and then sucked harder as she turned her chosen ones into her lovers.

The woman breathed through her mouth in short, quick bursts. Her body jerked as Amelia drained the blood from her throat. She knew to not drink too much, lest her lover die quickly and painfully. She took only what she needed – enough to render her lover helpless against her attraction.

Amelia found the zipper on the woman's dress. She slid the zipper down, and pulled the dress down over the woman's shoulders. It fell to the floor. The woman wore a black teddy beneath. Amelia felt her pussy moisten as she gazed at the lovely, lithe body. The woman pulled the teddy over her head, and laid it on the floor on top of the dress. She then pulled off her stockings and added them to the pile.

She stood before Amelia, naked and shivering in the cold. She heard people knocking on the door, calling to her to see if she was OK.

'I'm fine,' the woman called out. Amelia knew she told the truth. 'I'll be out in a few minutes.'

'Won't people want to come in here? You heard them knocking. We'll be caught,' the woman said to Amelia.

'Don't worry about them,' Amelia said. 'We won't be long here. We can take out time later tonight, away from the gallery. Now be quiet and let me make love to you.'

Amelia laid the woman down on the ground, over some canvas so she would not be lying on the cold floor. She lapped at the blood on the woman's neck. Her wound had stopped bleeding. Her hands found the woman's small breasts, and she kneaded one, then the other. She sank her teeth into the base of her left breast. The woman arched her back as Amelia sucked. Her nipples grew hard.

Amelia pinched them, which made her heart beat faster. Her blood flowed so quickly into Amelia's mouth that Amelia could not drink it all. She pressed her hand against the wound to stop the bleeding. As she lowered herself to the woman's thighs, she looked into her face, which was flushed yet pale from the loss of blood. There was longing in her expression. It was the familiar combination of longing and terror that Amelia had so often seen. She must be careful to not drain her dry. It would do no good to have a dead woman for a lover.

The woman lifted Amelia's face.

'Kiss my throat again, Hard,' she said. 'Tighten my scarf around my neck as you do it.'

Amelia's body flushed at what the woman wanted from her. Rarely did a lover like the suffocating feeling of blood being drained from the throat. She knew she could give the woman a monumental orgasm if she choked her gently. Amelia crawled up her naked body. She grabbed the scarf in her hands, and slowly tightened it. The woman moaned. Amelia moved the scarf so it was above the throat wound. She pulled it tightly, and once again sank her teeth into the woman's throat, feeling her heart pounding against her breasts as she did so. She pulled the scarf tighter, and the woman arched her back as she gasped in ecstasy. Amelia sucked more of her blood, tightening the scarf as she fed. The woman's eyes rolled back into her head. Her face was flushed from choking. Amelia held the scarf tightly with one hand, and slid the fingers of her free hand into the woman's bush. She found her labia and clitoris in no time. She massaged her clit until her legs stiffened. Two fingers reached inside, searched for her g-spot, and found it within seconds. Amelia massaged as she sucked. The woman's body went rigid. She held her breath. Then, her body uncoiled like a spring as an intense orgasm overcame her. She thrashed on the floor like a fish out of water. Amelia felt her pussy juices flow over her hand as she rubbed the woman's g-spot.

'Oh, God, don't stop,' the woman cried.

'I won't stop, Danielle,' Amelia spoke her name as she felt her climax flow over her fingers. 'Not unless you want me to.'

As Danielle's orgasm abated. Amelia let go of the scarf. She pressed her hand against Danielle's throat to stop the bleeding. She would be weak, but that was nothing a little linguine with clam sauce and Benedictine could not improve.

'I've never had an orgasm like that before,' Danielle said. 'Why on earth did I hate you so much?'

'You didn't hate me. You had no idea what to think of me. You're going to be a bit woozy for a few hours. Let's get you home and get some good food and liquor into you. Now dry your tears. There's nothing to be afraid of. You may still have guests outside.'

'Why ...? I don't understand. You wanted me the whole time?' Danielle asked.

'Yes. I like you angry. I like the energy. You thought I was taking Peter away from you. Not at all. As a matter of fact, I have some fun for us tonight.' Amelia grinned as she spoke.

Danielle dressed and tidied herself up while Amelia straightened out her dress. Danielle turned the gallery lights back on. Once the two women were ready, they emerged from the storage room. Two dozen people were left in the gallery. Peter stood near the door, and he gave them a quizzical look. Jeremy stood next to the refreshment table, sipping a glass of champagne. When he saw Amelia, he tipped his glass towards her in greeting.

She smiled at him. At her smile, he approached.

'Everything's OK. Danielle was just nervous over her first time,' Amelia smiled. She knew Jeremy and Peter thought she meant Danielle's first gallery opening, but both she and Danielle knew she meant something very different.

Danielle ran her fingers along Amelia's spine. Amelia felt her entire body melt.

'I have a bottle of wine chilling at our home, Peter. Roger is still here. He can keep the gallery open until closing. How about we invite Amelia and Jeremy over to our home?' Danielle said. She licked her new teeth. They had not grown in yet. She felt their electrical charge as they formed. She liked her new body and her new urges.

Amelia watched the two men, who had no idea what to make of these two women who had draped over one another after hating each other for so long. Amelia wanted to make Peter and Jeremy her own tonight, the same way she had made Danielle her own.

'I promise all of you we will have a delightful time,' Amelia said with a grin.

'I'm looking forward to it,' Peter said, not taking his eyes from Amelia. Jeremy smiled, and brushed his hand against Amelia's face.

'So am I,' Amelia said. 'Oh, so am I.'

Kicks
by Landon Dixon

She was standing on the sidewalk, in the rain. I slowed the car, pulled up to the curb. She was soaking wet, her white blouse and black skirt plastered to her body, like her black hair to her head. Her full breasts were on display through her now nearly see-through top, her rounded hips and flared thighs accentuated by the sodden skirt, long, stockinged legs pouring out the bottom and into a pair of shiny black high heels.

She was making no attempt to shield herself from the rain, like she'd given up trying, just standing next to the office building with a look of supreme frustration on her pretty face. Mascara streaked her cheeks, and her glossy lips were pressed tightly together.

It was well past office hours, but still fairly light out, despite the rain. I licked my lips, staring at the drenched and obviously abandoned woman, liking what I saw. I shifted the car into park and got out and ran over to her.

'You waiting for someone?'

She glared at me, her clear blue eyes flashing. 'Yeah, my fucking prick of a husband! You seen him?'

I grinned and shook my head, the rain splattering down on me. She was stunning up-close, dripping delicious, clothes clinging to her outrageous curves. 'He stood you up, huh?'

She snorted. 'He was supposed to pick me up an hour ago. But it's just like him to forget. He doesn't give a damn!' She held up her hands, her breasts rising in her soaked blouse. 'And now look at me!'

I was, enthralled. 'That's no way to treat a lady. Can I give you a lift somewhere?'

She stared at me, water running down her face and off the point of her chin. 'You want to give me a ride?'

'Yeah, sure. My car's right over there. Anywhere you want to go.' I smiled my most charming. I'm a stud by no means, but most women think I'm "cute", with my curly brown hair and dimpled chin and tight, compact body. I've been known to rescue a damsel in distress on occasions, as well.

'You really want to give me a ride? In place of my fuckingly thoughtless husband?'

'Yeah.'

She grabbed my arm, dragged me down the sidewalk and into an alley. She threw herself up against a slickened wall and pulled me in close. 'Well, ride me, Sir Galahad!' she hissed in my startled face. 'Fuck me, Prince Charming! Give it to me fast and furious in place of my fucking husband!'

I stared into her gleaming eyes. 'You want …'

She unzipped my jacket, pushed it back over my shoulders. 'I'm Megan. Fuck me!'

'Tony!' I blurted. 'Yes, ma'am.'

She tore my shirt open and thrust her hands inside, running her warm, damp palms over my bare stomach and up on to my chest. Clutching my pecs, she mashed her mouth against my gaping mouth, hungrily kissing me.

I surged with heat, gripping her buff shoulders and kissing her right back, her lips soft and wet, and demanding. The whole thing was so unexpected and spontaneous, uncontrollable. She wrapped her arms around my body inside my shirt and sucked on my mouth, chewed on my lips, her tits pressing hotly into my heaving chest.

The street was deserted and the alley empty, the warm rain washing down on us as we made out, inflaming our passions still more. She slid her hands down into the back of my pants and clawed at my butt cheeks with her sharp nails, as I pulled her blouse open at the shoulders, our mouths moving together.

'Yes!' she gasped, leaning back. Her blouse hung open to the cleavage, raindrops shimmering on her smooth, curved, white skin.

I gripped her blouse lower down and ripped it all the way open, sending ivory buttons rattling off the brick wall and clattering on to the pavement. Her tits were overflowing a satiny white bra, and I cupped them, squeezed them, revelling in their heft and heat. She squirmed up against the wall.

I wasn't responsible for my actions any more. I was on fire. She'd tempted me and I'd taken the bait; no man could hold it against me – not based on what she was offering. She popped her bulging bra open at the front and her tits sprung out into my clutching hands, bare and huge and soft.

'Suck them,' she rasped.

Her nipples were jutting pink exclamation points on the tremendous globes of her tits, and I dove my head down and took one into my mouth, sucked on it. She dug her fingers into my hair and pulled me in tighter to her chest, her breast-meat filling my mouth.

Someone ran by on the sidewalk. A shadow passed over the alley wall. But I paid no heed. I had my hands and mouth full, kneading Megan's tits, sucking on her nipples, my cock a pulsing length of steel in my pants.

'Oh, God, yes!' she moaned, writhing against the wall.

Then she jerked my head up and glared down into my eyes. 'I need you to fuck me. I want you to fuck me like my husband won't ever fuck me. Now!'

We scrambled my belt and fly open. She yanked my pants and shorts down, and my cock sprang up and out into the open. I gulped when the rain splashed against my throbbing shaft, groaned when Megan laced her long, slender fingers around it. She had me firmly in the palm of her hand.

She unhooked her skirt with her other hand and flung it aside, pulled her shiny white panties to one side. I stared down at the slick pink petals of her pussy, her hot, moist hand swirling up and down the pulsating length of my cock. 'Fuck me,' she breathed, sticking the bloated tip of my prick into her inner wetness.

I groaned, plunging into the woman's pussy. She clutched my bare ass and I moved my hips like she wanted, gliding my cock back and forth inside of her. We flailed our tongues together. She bit into my tongue, nails into my cheeks, driving me to fuck her harder, faster.

'Yes. Yes!' she screamed.

I pounded into her with reckless abandon, gripping her tits and bouncing her against the wall, churning her hot, wet, tight pussy. She was a complete stranger – a married woman – and we were out there fucking almost in the open in the pouring rain; and that made everything all the more exciting. Her tits jumped in my hands, body rocking against me. My balls tightened and tingled, cock flying.

'What the fuck?'

I jumped, twisted my head around.

A man was standing in the mouth of the alley, staring at us; a huge, angry-looking man. I tried to focus, still pistoning Megan's pussy in rhythm to her grasping hands.

'He got here first, asshole!' she snarled. 'You didn't show up, so I took what came along.'

My eyes and head began to clear. The hulking guy was Megan's husband. I was fucking his wife, right in front of him, my pumping cock gone come-hard in the woman's sucking twat.

'You're dead,' he growled at me, advancing on us.

Megan pulled one of my hands off her tits and thrust something cold into it – a gun. 'Shoot him! Kill the bastard,' she shrieked, undulating on the end of my prick.

I looked at the gun, at the man. He was almost right on top of us now, fury etched all over his face. Megan's pussy walls tightened on my cock, and I surged to the edge of coming, despite or because of the situation. I pointed the gun and pulled the trigger.

It clicked empty.

The man swatted it out of my hand, laughing.

'You'd kill for me. You'd actually kill for me,' Megan cooed.

Then she shoved me back so hard I popped out of her pussy and stumbled across the alley and slammed into the wall opposite. My cock bobbed obscenely stiff and pink, dripping.

'Am I a fucking temptress, or what, honey?' Megan said to her husband, holding up her arms and gyrating her wet, white body against the wall.

'You're some smoking hot bitch, all right,' he agreed, taking my place in between her legs and jamming his sledge of a cock into her slit. 'Thanks for the show, pal,' he sneered at me. 'And for warming my wife up.' He roughly gripped Megan's breasts and hammered her pussy.

She moaned, wrapping her arms around him.

I staggered over to the mouth of the alley, fumbling my cock back into my pants.

'Don't feel too bad, Tony,' she called after me, her voice jumping with the man's violent thrusts. 'We just do it for kicks!'

She hungrily kissed her husband, clutching his pumping ass.

It took a solid month of searching, but I finally found her again: standing by the side of a little-used road leading out of town.

The hot, glaring sun was beating down on her out there in the middle of nowhere, sweat glistening on her bare arms and legs and chest, loose black hair shining. She was wearing a blue top tied together under her breasts, a pair of tiny, torn jean shorts. Her tits swelled almost right out of the top, shorts hugging her hips and pussy tight.

I pulled the rented car off the shimmering asphalt and on to the dirt shoulder of the road, just beyond her. Then I adjusted my ball cap and sunglasses, the fake moustache pasted onto my upper lip, and backed the vehicle up so that I was directly across from Megan. 'Need a lift?' I asked through the open window, in a deeper voice than normal.

She slowly walked over and bent down and looked in the window, her breasts just about falling out of her top. 'My fucking husband was supposed to pick me up!' She glanced up and down the empty road, letting me get a good look at her luscious tits, her flat stomach and long, lithe legs. 'The fucking asshole!'

'Hot day to be standing out by the side of the road,' I said, flashing a grin.

She smiled back at me, her blue eyes sparkling. 'You're right there. Mind giving me a ride? Since my husband obviously isn't going to show up.'

'Love to.'

She opened the door and jumped inside the car, breasts jiggling, arms and legs flashing. 'I'm Megan,' she said, looking me over, paying particular attention to my bulging crotch.

'Anthony,' I responded, shifting into gear.

I barely had the car back on the pavement, when she reached over and grabbed on to the hard outline of my cock in my jeans. 'Why don't we teach that inconsiderate prick of a husband of mine a lesson, Anthony?' Megan suggested, rubbing my erection. 'That fucking asshole takes too much for granted.'

I grinned my agreement, warming in the heated palm of her hand.

She wet her plush, red lips. Then said, 'Turn off into those bushes up ahead.' She squeezed my pulsing cock, and I did exactly as she asked.

It was little more than a clump of trees, a picnic table, and a fire pit by the side of the road, but there was no one around, that I could see. I parked the car and we got out. And the black-haired beauty wasted no time, meeting me halfway around the vehicle and pushing me up against the trunk, pressing her burning-hot, perspiration-damp body into mine.

'I want you to fuck me!' she hissed in my face.

She kissed me, hard, her tongue invading my mouth and entwining around mine. I grabbed her tight, and she knocked my cap off, ran her fingers through my hair, undulating her tits and pussy against me. There was no resisting the woman.

We frenched furiously under the hot sun, along that deserted stretch of highway, feeling one another up. Until I spun Megan around and pushed her up against the trunk of the car, so she was facing away from me, gripping the hot metal. 'I'm going to fuck you like that prick of a husband won't ever fuck you,' I hissed in her ear, grinding my cock into her ass. Then sticking my tongue inside her ear, swirling it around.

She gasped and nodded, moving her taut, round bottom against my hard-on.

I unfastened her shorts and glided the skimpy garment over the glowing mounds of her buttocks and down her legs. There was no gun hidden in the back of her panties, because she wasn't wearing any panties. I smacked her lush cheeks, making the flesh ripple, as she pulled her top apart and flung it away.

I grabbed up her overripe bare tits from behind and squeezed them, pinched the stiffened pink nipples between my fingers, making her moan. Then I reached down and unzipped my jeans and pulled my swollen cock out, stuck it into the heated tunnel formed by her buttocks.

'You're sure your husband won't find you – come for you?' I whispered, kissing her neck, clutching her tits, frotting her ass.

'No,' she murmured, melting against me. 'He can go screw himself, for all I care.'

I kicked her legs apart and thrust my cock up into her pussy. We both groaned, rutting around out there in the open. I gripped her narrow waist and pumped my hips, sawing cock in and out of her dripping cunt.

Her fingernails scraped on the metal, as I rocked her back and forth with my prick. My thighs smacked against her bum, the wet sexual sound loud and clear in the still air.

As was the infuriated growl of, 'Hey, asshole, that's my wife you're screwing!'

I turned my head and stared at the huge, angry-looking

man emerging out of the bushes and striding towards us.

Megan bounced against me, fucking herself on my prong. 'He was here first, asshole!' she yelled at her husband.

I grinned at the guy, fast-fucking his wife.

He charged.

I drew my gun out of the back of my jeans and fired.

The first bullet whizzed past his ear and thunked into a tree, spitting bark. He stopped, stunned, Megan frozen in position on the end of my pole. The second bullet I sent shooting past his other ear, and he turned tail and ran, crashing through the underbrush.

'I guess he won't be bothering us any more,' I said, reholstering my smoking pistol, cock still embedded in Megan's pussy. I stripped off the shades and moustache, grasped the breathless woman under her armpits and pulled her up tight against me, revelling in the cool feel of her sweat, the trembling of her naked body.

Maybe they'd expected me to take a beating, while she watched, then had sex together. Or maybe they'd just hoped I'd make a humiliating run for it, cock tucked between my legs.

But now I groped Megan's tits and pumped her slit, fucking the other man's wife good and hard. She didn't say a word, her pussy gone even tighter, gripping my surging dong in a heated vice.

'What a kick, huh?' I grunted, pounding away at her. Then jerking, blasting my white-hot semen into the stunned woman over and over, thoroughly enjoying myself.

Forgotten Desires
by Tony Haynes

Sara fluttered her eyelashes at Marcus in what she hoped was a coquettish manner. 'Please?'

Marcus shook his head. He was adamant he wasn't going to give in to his wife.

Not to be deterred, Sara tried again. 'Pretty please?'

Marcus laughed. 'No!'

Sara crossed her arms and pretended to sulk.

'Aw don't be like that. We're nearly there. I just don't want to spoil the surprise, that's all.'

Sara's frown faded. She was only kidding. She leant across the hand brake and pecked her husband on the left cheek. 'If I didn't know any better I'd say we were going back to Uni.'

Marcus tensed.

His wife picked up on it straight away. She smacked him playfully on the left shoulder. 'We are! You rogue – you said you weren't ever interested in going to any old reunion events.'

'Well,' Marcus explained, 'it is the ten year anniversary of the night we first kissed. Unless you'd forgotten?'

'How could I?'

As Marcus turned off the main road and headed for the campus, Sara's heart began to race a touch faster as she recalled the night of the graduation ball. She often wondered if Marcus knew everything that had taken place that evening prior to their first kiss. A part of her felt excited at the prospect of seeing some of the old gang again, however she had mixed emotions at the thought of bumping into Luke and Alice.

Sara and Marcus checked into their old hall of residence, showered, changed and then made their way across to the student union bar, where the reunion event was being held. Though evening dress wasn't mandatory, nevertheless, Marcus had opted to wear his tuxedo. Thoughtfully, and a touch cheekily Sara thought, he had packed her favourite little black cocktail dress. Thankfully, it was one of those balmy summer evenings and so Sara was more than happy to wear it.

Upon entering the union bar Sara couldn't believe how many of her old alumni were there. As well as all of the people that she was in touch with on Facebook, there were also one or two people she had lost contact with who she was delighted to see again. In fact, Sara got so wrapped up in the evening she lost track of Marcus for a while as he disappeared off to hang out with some of his old rugby colleagues.

After about an hour Sara decided she had better try and seek out her errant husband. Looking around for Marcus, Sara thought she spied him at the bar, so headed on over. Carefully weaving her way through the throng, Sara came up behind the elegant figure in the dinner jacket and slid her hands around the front of his face in order to cover his eyes. 'Guess who,' she whispered.

'Hmmm, it might have been a while, but I reckon that's Sara Thompson.'

Sara gasped as Luke Harmon turned around and smiled

at her. She had forgotten how much he looked like her husband, especially from behind. She stumbled an apology, 'Sorry.'

'Don't be.' With that, Luke bent down and lightly brushed his lips against Sara's right cheek. Whilst it wasn't the first kiss of friendship that had been bestowed upon her that evening, somehow Sara felt as if this one was different. It seemed far more intimate for starters.

She glanced around and hoped that Marcus hadn't been watching. Thankfully there was no sign of him.

'So, what are you up to these days?' Luke asked.

Sara flashed her wedding ring by way of an explanation.

'Congratulations. Who's the lucky guy? Anyone I know?'

'Marcus,' Sara replied.

'Really?' Luke grinned. 'That calls for a celebration.' He turned and managed to grab a passing barman. 'Champagne please.'

Alas, being a typical student bar, there was none to be had, so Luke ordered the most expensive bottle of wine in the house instead – which still wasn't that expensive – and raised a toast to Sara.

After taking a sip of wine she asked the same question of him. 'And you?'

'Me what?'

'Are you married?'

'Engaged.'

'Not Alice surely?'

Luke winked. 'Now that'd be telling.'

As Luke took another sip from his glass of wine Marcus came up behind him. Marcus raised his right forefinger to his lips, beckoning Sara not to let on that he was there. Sara could feel the semblance of a smile tug at the corners of her mouth and she had to glance down so as not to give the game away. Marcus gently blew on the back of Luke's neck and whispered, 'Looking good Mr H.'

Luke spun around and found himself face to face with his old sparring partner. Just for a split second, Sara thought she spotted a look pass between them. The look made her wonder if Marcus knew she had kissed Luke earlier on the very evening that she and Marcus had first got together. The two men both grinned and then hugged in a rather laddish manner.

As they did so, Sara felt someone tap her left elbow. Even before she looked round Sara guessed it was the missing member of the quartet from that night all those years ago, the girl who had ended up with Luke, her best friend at the time, Alice. Sara had a sneaking suspicion that Alice had always had a big crush on Marcus. The foursome exchanged glances, then lapsed into a speculative silence. It was Alice who eventually broke it. 'It looks like we've got a lot of catching up to do.'

Sara found that the following couple of hours raced by as the four shared lots of laughs catching up on ten years worth of gossip. In fact, she could hardly believe it when last orders were called at the bar. Luke and Alice stood up.

'One for the road?' Marcus suggested.

'No thanks,' Alice replied. 'We quite fancy an early night.' Alice and Luke then kissed passionately. Even though it had been ten years Sara still remembered what a fabulous kisser Luke was. The four then bade one another goodnight and Luke and Alice disappeared.

When Marcus suggested they stay for a final drink, Sara declined. There was something about the way Luke and Alice had kissed she found extremely arousing and she wanted to get her man back to her room as quickly as possible, so they hastily drunk up and left the bar.

As Sara and Marcus made their way back across the campus grounds they decided to take a slight detour in order to wander past the block where they had once attended English lectures. They were about to round the corner of the building when they heard a faint rustling in the bushes over to their right. Thinking they might have stumbled upon a couple of old friends snogging, Sara suggested they sneak up on the pair and surprise them. Marcus thought it an excellent idea, so they crouched down and tiptoed towards the sound. As they rounded the corner they came upon a dense thicket. As Sara peered through the foliage her eyes widened in surprise, for the couple in question were far more intimately engaged than either Sara or Marcus had suspected.

It was obvious that Luke and Alice had come well prepared for their weekend away as they stood on a rather luxurious-looking car rug. They had clearly lost no time since leaving the bar for Luke was completely naked, apart from a flimsy pair of briefs which barely covered his hard on, whereas Alice was in the process of slipping out of her scarlet dress. As she slid the garment down her thighs and wriggled out of it, Sara remembered what a fine, voluptuous figure her friend had. Alice's gorgeous breasts looked as if they were ready to burst out of her sequinned bra. Eager to see the delights that hid inside, Luke reached around her back and unclipped it. Even in the moonlight, Sara could clearly see Alice's breasts. Luke cupped them in his hands and then leant down in order to kiss them, taking each in his mouth in turn. Alice's head lolled back and a gentle sigh escaped her lips. As he tended to her breasts, Alice reached down with her right hand and freed Luke's cock from his briefs. Taking a firm grip upon it she began to ease his foreskin back and forth.

Sara felt incredibly turned on as she watched the pair. She suddenly realised she wasn't the only one as she felt Marcus come up behind her and begin to nuzzle her neck. As he rubbed his groin against her, Sara could clearly feel his hard on pressing into her bottom. Marcus snaked his right hand around Sara's waist and ran it down the top of her thighs, searching for the hemline of her dress. When he eventually found it his hand inched the material upwards so as to allow him access to her skimpy black panties. Marcus wasted no time in wiggling them aside and slipping a finger into her pussy. Sara had to bite her bottom lip in order to stifle a low moan. It was sheer bliss to be pleasured by her man as she watched the scene between Alice and Luke unfold in front of her.

On looking back up, Sara saw Alice had taken her red thong off and was now lying down on her back. She opened her legs wide apart. Luke surprised his fiancée by licking the lips of her pussy before entering her. Alice thrilled, delightedly. The next second, Luke manoeuvred around until the tip of his cock nuzzled against the entrance to Alice's pussy. As he slid his cock inside Alice her mouth formed a silent 'O' of pleasure.

Sara could clearly see how turned on her old friend was. Little thrills of excitement pulsed between her own thighs and covered the middle finger of Marcus's right hand with sweet, sticky juice. Marcus withdrew it for a moment in order to taste her, only Sara beat him to it, took hold of his hand and guided it towards her own lips. Hungrily, she tasted herself as she licked the juice off. The second she released her grip Marcus returned the finger to its happy home.

By this time, Luke had built up a steady rhythm as he thrust in and out of Alice. The pair were patently both nearing their respective climaxes already. Their heavy breathing was clearly audible. Luke grasped the cheeks of Alice's bottom and sank deep inside her. Alice let out a yelp of delight as the pair came together.

Seeing the couple in such throes of ecstasy was too much for Sara and she sensed her own climax tingle between her thighs. She arched backwards against Marcus. He clasped her tightly to him as she came. Sara tried her best to remain silent, however she couldn't help letting out a tiny yelp of delight.

Alice and Luke glanced across in the direction of the sound. Luke withdrew from Alice enabling her to sit up. As she did so she called, 'Come out, come out whoever you are.' She took hold of her fiancé's cock in her left hand and held it up in an inviting manner. 'I have a present for you.'

Initially, Sara thought she and Marcus may have been able to simply sneak off, but as it was their old friends they decided to show themselves. They emerged from the bushes, both wearing slightly guilty looks, having being caught at playing voyeur.

'Well, well,' Alice said, 'It seems as if we weren't the only ones with the idea of an early night.' As she spoke, Alice continued to play with Luke's cock. She was fully aware that Sara was hardly able to take her eyes off it. Rather cheekily, Alice added, 'I don't suppose you fancy giving me a hand here?'

Sara glanced across at Marcus, seeking his approval before making any move. She realised she needn't have bothered, for Marcus was fixated by Alice's amazing tits. The warm summer night was suddenly alive with possibilities. Alice was the first one bold enough to suggest what they were all thinking. 'You remember our graduation night all those years ago? Don't you ever wonder what it might have been like if things had turned out differently?'

Sara and Marcus exchanged a knowing look and smiled at one another.

'I'm game if you are,' Sara said.

'Sounds good to me,' Marcus replied. They kissed passionately in order to seal the pact, then turned to face their respective new lovers.

Alice shook her head and tutted. 'First things first, let's get you out of those clothes.'

As Sara stepped towards Luke she got her second surprise of the night as he and Alice deftly swapped places.

'But ...' Sara began.

Alice held her left forefinger up to Sara's lips to stem the latter's protest. 'Ah-ha.'

Sara was about to object, but when she looked across at her husband she saw Luke was already in the process of slipping Marcus's dress shirt off, so Sara tried to steady her nerves, smiled at Alice and gave her friend a nod of approval. Alice looked delighted at being granted permission. Slowly, sensuously, she removed Sara's cocktail dress. As Sara stepped out of it, Alice ran her hands over Sara's lithe, firm body. With a swift, sleek move, Alice unhooked Sara's bra clasp with her right hand. As the bra fell to the floor, Sara instinctively reached up and covered her breasts. Alice pouted. Deciding she was being silly, Sara lowered her hands. Alice stood back for a second in order to admire Sara's pert little breasts. As she did so she whispered, 'You are beautiful you know.'

Sara wasn't sure how to respond. Words didn't seem

appropriate somehow so she leant forwards and planted the most delicate of kisses on Alice's lips. She'd never been intimate with another girl before. Alice's lips felt different to those of the men that she had kissed, they were softer and smoother. Upon parting, Alice smiled then glanced to her side. Naturally, Sara followed her friend's gaze. Sara gasped in surprise at what she saw, for Marcus and Luke were now both completely naked and locked in a tight embrace. As the two men parted they noticed their audience. Marcus looked slightly bashful as he explained, 'Well, we couldn't let you have all of the fun.' As he spoke, his left hand imperceptibly brushed Luke's cock. It twitched excitedly. Sara's gaze locked upon it once more.

'Swap?' Alice suggested

'I thought you'd never ask,' Marcus grinned.

Before the couples repositioned themselves, Alice whispered to Sara, 'What I'd really like is to see my fiancé's lovely thick cock plunging in and out of you.'

Sara's eyes lit up at Alice's comment. Just as she was about to pair off with Luke, Marcus drew her slightly to one side and asked her what Alice had said. When Sara told him, Marcus answered reassuringly, 'So would I.'

In spite of the endorsement, Sara felt shy as she approached Luke. He calmed her nerves by taking her in his arms and telling her if she didn't feel comfortable at any point, just to give him a nod. Acting much bolder than she actually felt, Sara squatted down and kissed the tip of Luke's cock by way of reply.

Luke practically fell on to the rug beside Sara and began to kiss her all over, his lips exploring every inch of her body. As Luke pleasured her, Sara looked across and saw that Alice had knelt down in order to take Marcus in her mouth. Sara was incredibly aroused by the sight of another woman's lips wrapped around her husband's cock. She was half tempted to wriggle around in order to suck Luke, only she never got the opportunity for the next moment she felt his delicious tongue delve into her pussy. Sara threw her head back in wild abandon, as Luke licked and toyed with her until her juices began to flow once more. Clearly aware of how aroused she had become, Luke broke away from Sara and asked if she would mind kneeling on all fours. Sara was only too happy too oblige. Gently, Luke then slipped his cock inside her. It didn't feel quite as long as Marcus's, but was maybe just a fraction thicker.

This position allowed Sara to watch her husband being sucked off by Alice as she was being fucked. It was simply the most amazing turn on of her life and when Alice winked at her friend, Sara nearly came right there and then. Sensing she was on the verge of orgasm, Luke slowed the pace at which he slid his cock in and out of Sara, allowing her to stave off her climax a moment or two longer.

As Sara glanced up, a naughty look spread across Alice's face. Alice withdrew Marcus from her mouth and beckoned him to step a touch closer to Sara, then kneel down. Marcus willingly obeyed. When they were within touching distance, Alice instructed Marcus to offer Sara his cock. Marcus was more than happy to do so. Eagerly, Sara clamped her lips around her husband's throbbing dick. The feeling was simply sensational, to have one cock easing in and out of her pussy and another between her lips.

Wishing to share the pleasure, Sara withdrew Marcus and offered his cock back to Alice. Alice proceeded to wank him off. Marcus closed his eyes. After being together with him for so many years, Sara read the telltale sign. Marcus sighed softly as creamy white spunk erupted from the end of his cock. Alice leant back and allowed it to splash against her tits. The sight of it proved far too much for Sara and she cried aloud as an incredible orgasm ripped through her.

Only when Sara was completely satisfied did Luke finally withdraw. Sara collapsed on the rug. Alice lay down beside her friend, took Sara in her arms and caressed her tenderly. The two girls kissed, then looked up at the two men. As Sara spotted that Luke's raging hard on hadn't abated in the slightest she eyed Alice steadily, 'Are you thinking what I'm thinking?'

There was a glint in Alice's eyes as she replied. 'Why Sara Thompson, I never realised what a bad girl you were.'

Sara wrinkled her nose at Alice. 'Neither did I.'

Marcus and Luke grinned at one another and began to kiss as Sara and Alice lay back and prepared to enjoy the show.

One-Way Swap
by Alex Jordaine

It was a fine day, bright and warm in the Californian sunshine, and Christine and Peter were both naked in the pool area. They were completely private there as the neighbouring properties were screened from view by the high wall that surrounded their garden. The sky above was clear apart from threads of thin clouds, and reflected sunlight danced on the shimmering water of the swimming pool. A solid bed of flowers presented a bright swathe of colour on the smooth lawn around it and a light breeze made the flowers tremble.

Christine, her shapely body tanned all over to a honeyed brown, was lying on her front on a sun lounger, basking in the afternoon sunshine. The beautiful brunette was resting her chin on her arms, and her eyes, which were shielded by sunglasses, were turned in the direction of the pool by her side where Peter was swimming. She watched as he dived to the bottom of the deep end and swam underwater, holding his breath. Peter broke surface near the edge of the pool right next to Christine's prone body. 'Put some suntan lotion on my back, would you please, darling,' she said.

'Sure,' her darkly handsome husband replied. He hauled himself out of the water, rivulets of water running down his tanned skin. Reaching out for a towel, he dried himself in a perfunctory way, rubbing quickly at his face and torso.

He dried his hands more thoroughly before picking up the bottle of suntan lotion. He poured some of it onto the palm of one hand and got to work. Folding his hands around and over Christine's shoulders, he kneaded the suntan lotion into her skin, smoothing her flesh with it. What a magnificent body she had, he thought as he worked his way slowly down her back: the swell of her beautiful breasts, her narrow waist, that gorgeous curvy rear: perfection.

Peter had thought once that he could never have enough of that wonderful voluptuous body. They had made love as much as they possibly could when they'd first met, he reminded himself, and that had been just the beginning. They had made love *all* the time when they'd been on honeymoon, lost to themselves in sensual delight. And when they weren't making love, they talked and talked: of books and films, of childhood and family and friends, of good times and bad, of dreams and fantasies. Their talk turned inevitably to sexual fantasies.

Like fucking each other's brains out at night time on the beach under the moon and the stars.

So that's what they did at midnight one night. The sandy beach was only a stone's throw from their holiday apartment and they rushed down to it, hardly able to contain their sexual excitement. Once there, they threw down their towels and stripped naked. Christine got on to all fours and told Peter to take her right there and then. Her pussy was hot and wet and tight as he pushed into her from behind, his cock forging deep into her. He pushed and pushed into the hot warmth of her sex, slick and oozing for him and she pushed and pushed back They thrust together hungrily on the warm sand, before plunging into the ocean itself and making love in the water in hopeless abandon as the waves crashed over them again and again, their only audience a crescent moon and the stars that glimmered above them in the endless sky.

And when they finally drifted back to the edge of the shore and back to their apartment and back to their bed Christine had wanted more. She said she couldn't help it, he'd made her insatiable. She had fallen onto Peter, grabbing his shoulders and making him lie on his back. She had raked her fingers over his smooth, hard body and then, her thighs pressing wetly against his, had guided him inside her. They went on to devour one another feverishly again. But eventually, inevitably, the fever turned into something else and their lovemaking became ever more languid and drowsily sensuous until sleep took them at last. And when they woke in the morning, locked in each other's arms, it started all over again. They couldn't resist going back to the beach at night either, most nights actually, to become one yet again with the elements in all their naked, uninhibited passion.

Their honeymoon had been a tough act to follow, Peter said to himself as he continued to massage Christine's back with suntan lotion. Even so, their lovemaking had carried on being almost as abandoned, almost as all-consuming, for a long time afterwards. They'd continued to trade sexual fantasies as well, fantasies that seemed to come from out of some murky dark nowhere in the mind. Christine said she fantasized about masturbating in front of him while he jerked off at the same time, and so they did just that, frequently.

Peter told her on one occasion – about two years into their marriage, it was – that he'd started having a recurrent fantasy of actually watching them making love. So, at his suggestion, they started fucking in front of their wardrobe mirror.

That was how it started, with that wardrobe mirror, innocuous really judged by all but the most puritanical of standards. But then things got more elaborate and they arranged – Peter's idea again – to have a mirror fitted to the ceiling above their bed.

What used to happen was this: Christine would straddle him – she liked that, she told him, being on top – and they would make love, with him watching her in the ceiling mirror and her looking down at him. She said she liked that too, loved it, said it gave her such a feeling of control.

Peter remembered her saying that. Christine remembered it too. She remembered it all. She remembered how he would sigh and let his body collapse into submission as she straddled him, pressing her groin on his, and how she would moan with pleasure as she felt the thickness of his cock slide into her pussy, so tight and moist. She remembered how Peter would reach up to her and she would grab his arms and pin them above his head. She remembered how he would groan with her movements as she pushed her hips down, fitting them around his hardness. She remembered the short, throaty cry Peter would let out, looking up at the mirror in the ceiling as he watched her grinding into him. He could see it all in the mirror.

Christine could see it all too now in her mind: the expression on Peter's face when she looked down through half-drawn lids at him, the wonder in his eyes and his slack, open mouth. She could hear it all too, and feel it: how when she shoved herself down on him with force, he gave out a soft groan and whimper and would stiffen even more inside her.

Then Christine would grip his arms more tightly and push her weight forward, falling down on him, whilst still moving her hips, so that the pressure on them both remained unabated.

And she could smell it now too, smell the scent of his excitement and sweat as he began a long drawn-out moan and started to thrust his hips up rhythmically, pulsing with a climax she knew he'd do his very best to restrain until she'd had her own orgasmic release.

Christine remembered that at this point she would begin to moan and flush and rock back and forth, so conscious of Peter's stiffness steely-hard inside her and ready to burst, and her hand would start to rub out a complementary rhythm, sticky and frantic, over her stiff clitoris. Then she would let go of herself altogether and shudder frenziedly as exquisite oscillations began to pulse through her. And as she climaxed she would watch his mouth widening in exaltation as, taken along by her orgasm, he allowed himself his release. He would begin to tremble uncontrollably beneath her before shooting his liquid, spurt after vigorous spurt, deep inside her sex.

Peter finished massaging Christine's back with suntan lotion and plunged back into the swimming pool with a splash. Christine stayed where she was on the lounger, alone with her thoughts once more, and her memory leapt back three years almost to the day. That was when Peter had told her he had another fantasy, one he just couldn't get out of his mind: a fantasy, "now don't be shocked, Christine", of seeing her fucking someone else.

But surprise, surprise, she hadn't been shocked, far from it. The idea turned her on too, she had to admit it, turned her on a hell of a lot. And they were a broadminded couple, a liberated couple, a couple that made their fantasies a reality, weren't they? You bet your sweet life they were.

Christine and Peter got rid of the ceiling mirror, bored with that now anyway. They arranged to have another mirror rigged up – a large one-way mirror this time, between their bedroom and the one adjacent to it.

Everything was all set for the big event.

They say you always remember the first time. Christine certainly remembered the first time she picked up a stranger to have sex with, knowing that her husband would be watching it all from the next room and jerking off.

What had been his name now, that first one: Jay was it, Jake? Fucked if she could remember. But she could remember the fuck. In fact she could vividly recall the sharp, nasty thrill of the whole experience from start to finish.

She remembered what she'd been wearing, or nearly wearing, when she'd picked him up at the bar. It had been a diaphanous little dress that was cut indecently high on the thigh and low over her breasts. She wasn't wearing any underwear either, as was her wont. She had on strapped black sandals with very high heels as well, to complete her fuck-me ensemble.

Christine couldn't remember what he'd been wearing, this Jay, Jake whoever, only that he'd been tall, well-muscled and handsome with longish, raven-black hair. She remembered kicking her shoes off as soon as they'd entered the bedroom, pulling her miniscule dress over her head; remembered telling him to get naked too and put on the condom she was now handing him. She remembered pushing him down on to the big bed after he'd done that and straddling him, positioning herself so she could manoeuvre the head of his cock against her pussy lips, against her clitoris. She remembered rubbing herself against his cockhead gently at first and then more vigorously, making him breathe heavily with sexual arousal.

She remembered sliding herself onto his shaft right up to the hilt, and then up and down, up and down, on and on. She remembered riding him in a mounting frenzy of lust, the blood pounding in her veins, until she was completely absorbed in the pleasure she was giving herself and the pleasure she was giving to the man behind the one-way mirror.

'Was it good for you?' she said when it was all over.

'The best,' sighed her companion as he lay spent and damp on the rumpled sheets. But Christine hadn't been talking to him, the sex machine she'd just used, the human dildo. She'd been looking in the mirror, *through* the mirror to the person she'd really been making love to.

That had been three years ago now. Since then she'd let Peter watch her having sex with a host of other strangers. It was what he said he wanted. But Christine wanted it too, make no mistake, wanted it in her imagination and wanted it in reality too. That was the number one rule from her point of view: she had to really want it. If she did it meant she was in control, which was crucial. But Peter said he liked to be in control as well, and he got his wish also for, as he was fond of saying, what person is more in control than the masturbator?

Which was essentially what Peter became from that first time, because from then on he and Christine seldom made love together. Instead they played out this kinky surrogate ritual with ever more frequency, both coming to crave it like a powerful drug, and enjoying it immensely too, each time they did it. And Christine simply *loved* to give Peter something really worth watching – worth wanking over. She would always put on as good a show as possible for him.

She would put on an especially good show for him tonight, Christine told herself as she continued to bask in the sunshine by the side of the rippling pool. But you never knew for sure how things would go with one-night stands. After all it took two to tango, as the saying went. Actually sometimes – tonight as it turned out – it took more than two ...

When Christine walked into the bedroom with the two hunky blond guys that she'd picked up not half an hour ago in a nearby bar, she knew one thing for sure. She knew that Peter would have already started stroking his cock with practised ease behind that one-way mirror.

She knew – and the knowledge of it made her clit twitch, made her sex feel slippery – that he'd be masturbating with a little more vigour now she was peeling off her tight top and micro-mini skirt and slipping out of her high heeled shoes. It obviously really turned on the two chiselled hunks she was with to discover she hadn't been wearing a stitch of underwear beneath that sexy outfit and that her breasts were soft but firm and her nipples stone-hard and her pussy completely shaved. Christine knew the fact that she was clearly turning them on would have turned on her husband as well. She knew he would be masturbating even more vigorously at the sight of her as she cupped her breasts and rolled her stiff nipples between her fingers.

'Strip for me,' Christine said and she knew that *he* knew that instruction *wasn't* for him, knew that she knew he was already stark naked and wanking. The two blond studs were also naked now, their muscular bodies looking as if they'd been sculpted of creamy tan stone, their cocks thickly inflated. Christine saw herself in the mirror as she knew her husband could see her at this stage of the show, her head back and her full lips parted as those two beautiful specimens of manhood fed hungrily on her breasts, suckled her engorged nipples.

She knew that Peter would be stroking his cock even more energetically by now, pulling and gasping, as he witnessed the three-way scene unfolding before his eyes. She knew he'd be working his fist up and down ever more insistently as he watched his raunchy, exhibitionistic wife drop to her knees and grab a cock in each hand. Christine stroked the guys' hard-ons, glancing lustfully from one stiff cock to the other, then into the mirror, imagining that all-important third cock being pulled up and down, up and down, faster and faster.

Christine's eyes gleamed and she smiled a salacious smile to the man behind the one-way mirror before putting one of the hunky strangers' hard cocks into her mouth. She sucked on it for a while, as she held on to the man's buttocks, at one moment pulling him in, at another controlling the movement so that it was smooth and fluid. And then she did the same to the other cock. Christine alternated between the two hard cocks, sucking expertly on each in turn, before jamming both of them into her mouth at once. She bet Peter almost shot his load when he saw her do that. But she knew that a highly experienced voyeur like him wouldn't have actually ejaculated. She knew that Peter would be wanking away hard, without doubt, but that he would make damn sure he didn't spill his seed until he'd seen all there was to see.

Christine finally disgorged the two cocks, withdrawing them slowly from her mouth, and got back to her feet. She handed each man a condom and told them to put them on.

Once they'd done that she pushed one of the men down on to the bed and climbed on top of him, steering his swollen cock into her pussy and making him groan with pleasure. And as he started sliding his shaft in and out of her dripping sex, forging deep into her, she reached back and spread the cheeks of her backside. Christine looked at the second man. 'There's a bottle of lube on the bedside table,' she said. 'Lubricate your cock and my asshole and then butt-fuck me.'

'Will do,' the man replied excitedly, thoroughly dousing his shaft and her anus with lube and then climbing into position. Christine reached back again, this time to fold her hand around his lubed-up erection. She rubbed the slippery head against the equally slippery opening of her anus and then let the man ease his shaft into her until it ground at the back of her rectum. And her anal hole was so tight around his cock that she felt her pussy tighten too around the other guy's cock, which was pounding into her wet, humid sex. Then the man behind her really started pounding too, ramming into her anus hard and fast.

It felt so good to Christine to be penetrated front and rear like that, felt even better to know her voyeuristic husband could see it all and would be pulling at his cock furiously now, his fist working up and down faster and faster. Christine loved being fucked in both holes at the same time, loved it all the more knowing she was being watched by Peter as she was being fucked that way. She knew as he witnessed the three-way spectacle she'd laid on for him he would now be jerking away at his cock like a jack-hammer.

Christine decided it was time to bring the show to its grand finale. She ground her hips down, churning her pussy back and forth on the throbbing cock of the guy beneath her until he suddenly opened his mouth, let out a moan and came hard. His body shook as he grasped Christine's waist and ejaculated, and that brought even closer the impending orgasm of the man hammering into her anus. He speeded up his thrusts, butt-fucking her in a frenzy as she pushed herself back on him until he was jolted by a shuddering orgasm.

Then Christine was overcome herself, and her glistening body quivered uncontrollably as she came right along with her husband. Because she knew, just *knew* that Peter was shooting warm, silky sperm all over his fist at that very moment as he joined in the climax of the *four*-way fuckfest that had been her special gift to him ... and to herself.

Deeds of Mercy
by Giselle Renarde

If Mercedes had to sum up her ridiculously complex sex-life, it would go something like this: she used to date an older guy named Simon, who was all the while married to a woman called Florence. After years of hope and heartbreak, Mercedes broke it off with Simon and ultimately found herself engaged to a young guy named Anwar. Things were pretty solid until Mercedes met up with Simon again, purely by chance. She had no intention of hooking up with him ... until he made her an offer of cold, hard cash! With Mercedes' love of secrets, cocks, and infidelity, how could she refuse?

Mercedes' romantic world had grown into a man-eating monstrosity. She pictured it looking a lot like that giant plant from *Little Shop of Horrors*. She couldn't say why she kept seeing Simon. She really did love Anwar. It wasn't that she needed the money. Well, OK, the money was nice and it gave her a cheap thrill every time she added Sex-with-Simon cash to the Wedding-with-Anwar fund, but it's not like she was living at subsistence level. She didn't *need* it. But she liked it. She enjoyed the naughty thrill of prostituting herself to her married ex-lover while her husband-to-be remained oblivious.

Simon was very different as a paying customer than he'd been back when Mercedes was simply his doting mistress. He'd been so careful before. Now he took all sorts of chances. He didn't seem to give a fuck about getting caught. Maybe that was a product of now being able to say, 'What, this chick? I'm just paying her to suck my balls. Don't feel threatened, wifey.' Mercedes was sure the money made all the difference.

In the four years of their "couplehood", such as it was, Mercedes had never seen Simon's house. Never. She'd never seen his wife or his grown children, live in person or via any other medium. They'd been names, nothing more. In fact, his entire family was off-limits to her, though the rule itself remained unspoken.

That was then. Now, when Florence left town to visit her relatives for the weekend, Simon insisted Mercedes stay the night.

'At your house?' she asked.

'At my house,' he replied.

'But ...' Mercedes couldn't seem to locate the words required to express her trepidation. She wasn't even sure what precisely she was worried about. 'A whole night? That's ... a lot of hours. And we'll be ... sleeping ... together?'

Even over the phone, Simon sounded peeved. 'The whole time we were together, you begged me to spend the night with you. Now you don't want to?' He let out a *humph* and then said, 'I'll pay you per hour of sleep, if that's what you're so worried about.'

'No, no. I mean, yes, thank you, but ...' It finally clicked why she shouldn't be spending nights with her ex. 'Anwar! What am I supposed to tell Anwar?'

'Are you suddenly living together?' Simon asked in his rhetorical voice. 'No? Then what difference does it make where you sleep?'

Setting emotion aside, Mercedes looked at the situation

from a business perspective: she could either spend Saturday night falling asleep in front of Anwar's TV, or go to Simon's house, get fucked, get paid, go to sleep, get paid, and probably get fucked and paid once again come morning.

'OK,' she said. 'You're right. I'll make it work.'

With a simple lie about a girls' night, Mercy set off to visit Simon's house for the first time. Her stomach tied itself in knots. She felt strange, knowing she'd be fucking some woman named Florence's husband in said woman named Florence's house. She felt sleazy about it. *Florence*. What an old lady name. Who was this woman named Florence? And why had Mercedes never wondered about her before now? Why did Simon cheat? Did this woman drive him to it? Was she horrible? Demeaning? Rubbish in bed? That must be it. Why else would Simon pay Mercedes for sex?

When she arrived at his door, Mercy expected Simon to grab her by the arm and swoop her inside, whispering, 'Did the neighbours see you?' Well, that wasn't how it went down. Simon opened the door, casting a dark shadow across the stoop. He looked her up and down. Even as a dog-walking couple sauntered along the sidewalk, Simon smiled and told her she looked good enough to eat.

'I hope so,' she mumbled as she crept inside.

She thought she'd be curious about this house of Simon's, but her present feeling was exactly the opposite of curiosity. Mercedes tried not to look anywhere or see anything. Her senses dulled as he guided her by the arm. She stared down at her stocking feet against dark hardwood floors. Where were her shoes? She must have taken them off without realising.

There were pictures on the walls, but Mercedes

wouldn't allow herself to look at them, not even to distinguish whether they were paintings or photographs. Why had she come here? Business, pleasure, or pure masochism?

Soon, they came to be in a bedroom on the second floor of the house. When had they ascended a staircase? Mercy's mind was muddled with desire for absentia intermingled with desire for Simon. Despite her best efforts to find the man unattractive, she couldn't help being drawn to a body that defied age. Simon was always hard before his pants hit the ground, and his erections were thick and firm. When he fucked her, she always left satisfied. Better than satisfied, in fact ... swollen and wet, sore and gasping for breath.

Now he seemed to be undressing her. No, scratch that. He seemed to have *undressed* her. Mercy's clothing hung over the back of a chair by the wooden desk. He was undressed too, but his clothes were on the floor. As always, his erection shot out in front of him like it was dowsing for wetness. Yes, Mercy realised, she was dripping for him. *Dripping*.

Simon's hard cock swung from side to side as he strutted to the bedroom door and closed it. His body gleamed golden in the low light of two bedside lamps, which cast Mercy's shadow up against the adjacent wall. The room was stark, she noticed. But she didn't want to notice – anything – so she focused her attention on Simon. 'How do you want me?' she asked.

He could do anything to her. They'd agreed on a flat rate for any activity, except for the hours of sleep, which would cost extra. He usually started with a blowjob and finished off fucking her pussy. On rare occasions he fucked her ass, but he knew that hurt her and she really didn't like it all that much.

'I want to eat you,' he said. His forceful gaze burned like the glowing embers in the gas fireplace across from the bed. 'I miss the taste of your cunt. I want you on my tongue.'

That statement should have excited her, but Mercy was too entranced by the fireplace. It seemed brand new. Why would a couple with a lousy sex life get a gas fireplace installed in their bedroom? It wouldn't be for heat. There were plenty of other ways to heat up a bedroom. *God!* Simon and his wife couldn't possibly have a healthy sex life, could they? If they did, why did Simon have an affair with Mercedes? Why was he now paying her for the pleasure of eating her pussy? But what reason other than romance was there for a new fireplace in a bedroom?

Simon lifted her off her feet and dropped her on the bed. She bounced. The quilt was too pretty to mess up with her juices, but it was too late now. As Simon crawled up from the base of the bed, snarling like a wild thing, Mercy felt her inner thighs drench with juice. She crept back from him and drowned in a multitude of pillows. There was nowhere left to go. Only a wooden headboard remained at her back. Simon smiled in a sneering sort of way. 'Where are you going, Mercy? I thought you wanted me to eat you.'

'I do,' she said. Her heart fluttered as he grabbed her ankles and pulled her legs wide open.

'Nice work if you can get it,' he teased as he propelled his body between her legs like a trench soldier. 'You just sit back and enjoy my tongue on your pussy, and then you go home with your bra stuffed with cash. Wish I could find a job like that.'

His smugness would have pissed her off a few years ago. Now it turned her on. She couldn't bring herself to play the possession. 'It's too late for you,' she replied.

'Gotta be young and beautiful for a sweet position like this.'

'Sweet position?' Simon chuckled as he dove between her thighs. He went right at it and obviously didn't plan on letting up until she came hard enough to wake the neighbours. Back when they were a "couple", he'd been so dainty about eating her. He'd give her clit a few licks, she'd pretend he was God's gift, and then they'd move on to something else.

This was something else altogether. Simon was like a different person now he was paying for sexual gratification. He tore into her like a beast. Holding her thighs wide apart, he pressed his face firm against her pussy so his lips met her clit and his nose planted in her trimmed bush. Mercy could feel the stubble on his chin against the base of her wet slit. His bristled cheeks scratched her outer lips like pleasant sadists as he took her clit in his hot mouth.

Mercy's whole body jumped. Simon sucked her clit like it was a tiny cock. This was something she'd never experienced before. Where had Simon picked up new material? Was it something his wife had taught him? No, couldn't be. Mercy was convinced they had next to no sex life. She'd convinced herself.

Sensation melted Mercy's mind. She bucked against Simon's face. Now she knew why guys got off on blowjobs. As Simon sucked her inner lips in with her clit, she tossed her head back and grabbed his with both hands. She thrust her hips at his face until she felt the scratch of his whiskers against her slit. His nose was flush to her bush. Could he even breathe down there? Mercy didn't give a fuck. She ran her pussy in tight circles against his muzzle. The prickle against her tender flesh generated an itch to fuck, and she hoped he'd get his cock inside her soon.

She'd have to come first, of course, but that was no chore. The harder Simon sucked her clit, the harder it became to resist giving herself over to the looming wave of climax. She forced her clit into his mouth, nearly sitting upright as he splayed himself belly-down on the bed. With his head in her hands, she pushed his face against her pussy the way porn star men do to porn star women when they're getting their blowjobs. She felt almost guilty to treat him this way, especially when he'd be paying her in the morning, but she was so close to coming she couldn't stop now.

Finally, the urge to move was subsumed by the urge to receive pleasure. Mercy held Simon's face against her pussy and screamed as he sucked her like mad.

When she finished screaming and could take no more pleasure or pain, Mercy closed up her legs and fell back into the cluster of pillows. Either her eyes were closed or she'd just gone blind. Her orgasm had so overtaken her she couldn't figure out which was the case. She finally realised her eyes were indeed closed, and she decided to open them. When she did, she saw two things: Simon looming between her knees with his long cock looking like it wanted to get up inside her, and, on the mantle behind him, a wedding photo. She must only have spent a few seconds looking at it, but she recognised a youthful Simon as the groom. The woman in the white gown was obviously his bride.

Mercy was shocked by this photo. Not because it was a wedding photo – she obviously knew Simon was married. This photo told her one thing she'd never known about the man: his wife was pug fugly. Worse than pug fugly! She had a face like a bulldog after a bar brawl. And in her wedding photo! A woman always looked her best on her wedding day. If Florence looked like that when she was married, imagine what she must look like now!

'I want to fuck you,' Simon growled. Slipping off the bed, he flipped her from her back to her front. 'I want it doggie style.'

'Yeah.' She felt too distracted to sound sexy. And then her gaze fell to another photo. This one sat on the night table right beside Mercy's face. It was definitely Florence – the face was an older, more wrinkled, even uglier version of the one on the mantle. She looked like a Halloween hag. Could this really be Simon's wife? Christ, no wonder he was willing to pay Mercedes for sex!

As Mercy lay staring at the figure in the photo, Simon climbed on the bed and splayed her legs as far apart as they would go. That action jolted her into the moment. Her pussy clenched in anticipation. She closed her eyes, but the image of Simon's ugly wife seemed burnt into her retinas.

When Simon grabbed her hips, Mercy raised her ass to him. He knew exactly what he wanted these days, and he lifted her up to the perfect height. After piling up pillows under her pelvis, he wasted no time going at her. He rammed her so hard it panged inside, but Mercy didn't care. The pang of a gleaming purple cockhead against her insides hurt less than the sting of resentment in knowing what Simon had stayed with throughout their years together.

He scratched her back with sharp little nails as he fucked her pussy. The pain felt wonderful. He smacked her ass cheeks until they turned red. That felt even better. But why had Simon stayed with such an ugly woman when he could have had Mercedes? As his cock raced in and out of her hot, wet pussy, Mercy realised how ridiculously narcissistic she was being. Maybe Florence was the nicest, sweetest, most internally beautiful person in the world! Maybe Simon had a thousand reasons to stay married to her.

Grunting like a troll, Simon threw his sweating chest on top of Mercy's back. The pillows piled underneath her pelvis held their butts aloft, but Simon grasped her wrists and held them down as he fucked her. She felt trapped in his body now, as her mind was trapped in a cycle of, "Why her and not me? Why choose ugly when he could have beautiful? What's so great about Florence?"

Even as Simon grabbed Mercy's breasts and groaned, the pleasure of fucking couldn't dispel the multitude of questions. Simon propelled his hips at Mercy's ass and bit down hard on her shoulder. Mercy screeched. Pain soared through her body. Her blood sizzled in her veins. She was sweating all over this pretty marriage quilt, and her pussy juice now graced a stack of throw pillows. As her cunt clamped down on Simon's orgasmic cock, a series of words tumbled out of her mouth unhindered, 'My God, Simon, your wife is one pug ugly motherfucker!'

The room went silent as Simon rolled off Mercy's back. The bed bounced beneath them. Was there any utterance crueller than the one that had just passed her lips? She'd insulted Simon's wife! This was the woman he'd been married to for how many years? And Mercy called her ugly. Why would she say that? Was she jealous? Even with her engagement to Anwar, was she still subconsciously coveting Simon? Was she still in love with him? Or was this wife of his simply unconscionably ugly?

'God, I know she is,' he finally said. 'And she always was. It's embarrassing, isn't it?'

With a growl, Simon pulled Mercedes down from her Princess-and-the-Pea stack of pillows. Tossing her on to her back, he rolled on top. His spent cock drooled forgotten spurts of come against her leg as he took her breast in his mouth and sucked. Everything he did to her was animalistic now. There was an intangible sort of brutality in his every move.

After a moment of vicious nipple sucking, Mercedes asked, 'Why did you marry her?'

Simon pressed Mercedes' breasts together. When he spoke, his voice resonated from somewhere inside her cleavage. 'Back in the day, she used to be great in the sack.' He laughed, and collapsed beside her on the bed. Grabbing a pillow for his head, he squeezed her in close to his body and closed his eyes. 'Same reason I stick with you.'

Mercy's heart froze in her chest. When Simon pressed a cruel kiss against her temple, she tried to ease herself away, but he only wrapped her tighter in his arms. The implications were too many, and too jarring. Her mind raced. Sure, he was paying her to stay the night, but Mercedes didn't sleep a wink.

Pattie and Annette
by Penelope Friday

John leans back in his chair and takes a sip of his beer, looking at the beautiful brunette opposite him.

'Love me, love my girlfriend. Simple as that.

'See, my girlfriend and me, we're close. She's my Primary and always will be; she's my girl, my love. We've been together – oh, a couple of years now? Something like that. Doesn't stop me fancying anyone else – doesn't stop me fucking anyone else. But say one word against my girl and you're out of here. Not only am I not prepared to fuck around behind her back, I'm not having anything to do with anyone – *anyone* – she doesn't like. OK?'

He smiles at his companion and runs a hand through his hair in an almost embarrassed gesture.

'OK. You're still here. That's a good start. Most people walk out before I've got halfway through the spiel. And yes, by the way, I've seen you looking. At her, I mean – not at me. *I'm* not exclusive, either. I'm not some tosser who thinks there's one rule for me and another for my girl. If she fancies you, you can go ahead with my blessing. And hopefully with me looking on, though that's not required either. Bloody damn hot, though, you and the chick going at it. Not sure I wouldn't prefer watching that to having you myself. Two hot chicks together? Whoa, man. Sounds good to me. And I'm pretty sure it'd look even better.

'What's my name? I'm John. And my girlfriend's Pattie. No, don't go there with the euphemisms – both of us have heard 'em all before. After a bit it just gets fucking annoying, you know? That's her, over there – blonde, gorgeous, gorgeous breasts and a mouth just made for kissing. She'll join us in a minute. But anyway, let's talk about you. Annette, your name is? Sweet Annette, a perfect name for a perfect lady. You've got beautiful ... eyes. No, really, I mean it. Dark brown, and looking like you can see right through me.

'Looking like you like what you see.

'Oh, babe. Look, I'll be honest with you. I can't believe that Pattie wants me, let alone that anyone else would. And that's not meant to be derogatory to Pattie, just that we've been together so long that I've had to accept that in her eyes, I'm not unfanciable.'

He smiles at the blonde, now sitting on his right at their table; gives her a bit of a wink, then blows her a kiss. Before he starts speaking again, he takes another gulp of his beer.

'Pattie, see – she makes me feel like I'm not the most ugly guy in the world. I'm not someone who girls will look at and go, "you must be joking – no one in their right minds would want you".

Hell, I know I was coming on strong a minute ago, but that was because I reckoned you would walk away. After all, why would a girl like you go for a guy like me? I'm not fishing here, by the way. If you want to turn round and say, "I'd fuck Pattie, but not you in a million years", that's OK by me. Well, if it's OK by Pattie, of course.' He looks enquiringly at the blonde. 'Yes? Yeah well, I'm not surprised you want her, Pattie. Who wouldn't?' He turns back to his other companion. 'Because you, lady. You're hot. I shouldn't say it, but look around this whole city, and you could pull anyone you fucking pleased. And you'd fucking please them, I can tell you.'

He leans forward towards her.

'Oh God, I just died and went to heaven. Tell me you said it. Tell me you said you'd have me and Pattie in turns. I'm imagining stuff, right? It's OK, that's fine. I can cope with that if I have to. You can tell me you never said any such thing. That you wouldn't let me see Pattie sucking your small, gorgeous breasts, biting down – just a little – on your nipples so you moaned in mingled pleasure and pain. That I couldn't see you squirming beneath me as I fucked you to heaven and back.

'I'm dead. I'm totally dead. I'm thinking about you climbing the stairs in our apartment and I'm thinking there's no way this is happening. I'm looking the way your high heels make your legs look so fucking long, and there's this place – this wonderful place – where they disappear into that short pink skirt of yours, and you don't know how much I'm dying to lick my way up from your shiny shoes till I'm right beneath your skirt. Don't tell me if you've got knickers on or not. I don't want to know. I want to imagine.

'I want to imagine licking and sucking my way up your body while Pattie licks her way down. Fuck, I'm hard, thinking of that. We'd meet on your belly button, my mouth full of your cream and hers tasting of your breasts. You can take us in turns after that; I want to watch you sucking Pattie till she comes, so you can listen to her scream for you and feel hotter than ever. Then I want to see Pattie with her fingers inside you making you buck and beg for more. You look such a bloody lady; I want to hear you cursing and swearing and pleading with

Pattie to fuck you harder, fuck you more. I want to watch every fucking gorgeous second of it, see you all sweaty with your long hair sticking to your face, with your eyes so full of desire and lust.'

John sighs, the vision going through his head as if it were actually happening now, right in front of him.

'And then. And then, oh baby. Then I'll get my turn with you. I'll be able to slide my cock inside you, as slippery as you are from Pattie's attentions. I can push right in, right in really deep, further than Pattie's fingers could reach. So you feel so ... so full. So wanting. And then I'll start moving. In and out. I'll flip you on to your front and watch your breasts bouncing as we do it doggie style. You'll put a hand between your legs to fondle your clit; and Pattie will move in and offer to do it for you. And you'll say yes. So many times *yes* to have Pattie touching you there as I thrust in and out of your gorgeous pussy. You'll want to kiss her but you won't be able to because you'll be panting out your need. You'll know Pattie is watching you and you'll want to put on a show for her because she's worth it. You'll want it never to end. Hell, *I'll* want it never to end. But with Pattie's hand between your legs, with my cock inside you – you'll scream and come and push me over the edge till my cock twitches and thrusts inside you, spilling my come all into your gorgeous body.'

John takes a deep breath, and reaches out to touch the brunette's hand. Then, smiling, he reaches the other hand out to Pattie, and strokes her arm gently.

'My girls. My beautiful, gorgeous girls. I'm imagining you coming upstairs with me. To let yourselves *come* upstairs. Both of you together, each in turn, whatever you want. Over and over, as many times as you want. With each other, with me, just watching. So many times you're begging that we stop, telling us that you'll die from the pleasure. Hey, babe, Annette – look at my girl, my Pattie – look at her beautiful curves, her rounded arse which says "fuck me" in any language you know. Don't you want her so bad? Imagine her kissing you, slipping her tongue between your lips and pulling you into her so your breasts rub together, your nipples slide into sharp points of need. Think of me watching, so fucking hard I don't dare touch myself in case I come before you've even got started with me.'

John shifts in his seat, his erection digging into him as he follows his own train of thought. He lets go of the girls, and rubs a hand across his groin, enjoying the tingling sensation; enjoying torturing himself by just talking. The wait is part of it. Teasing himself by refusing to let go, refusing to go upstairs quite yet. He's got so much more to say to Annette before the action starts. So many ideas. So many things he wants to share with her.

'Then, gorgeous, think of what I want to do to you, after Pattie's finished. Think of me fucking Pattie later, smelling your scent on her as I do so, remembering how you looked as she took you – how you looked as *I* took you. Imagine that, babe. You're hot. You're so damn hot.'

He takes a breath.

'You don't know how gorgeous you are, do you? You think you're too slim. You think the glasses make people think you're intellectual, not fuckable. Babe, I think you're both. No, scratch that. I know you're both. Those idiots who can't see past your quietness, who call you stuck up because you don't say much – that's what they are, just idiots. I look at you and see a gorgeous woman, someone I'd love to spend time with. You're a sweet person, as well as being drop dead lovely. I mean it. Pattie reckons so too, don't you, babe?'

John looks across at the blonde, and gives her another smile. Pattie doesn't know how much she changed his life when she came into it. She doesn't realise how much she's given John, but he knows. He knows, and loves her for it. And now he's going to have Annette, too. He's so fucking lucky.

'So, we'll fuck until we have to stop – every which way we can. And then, babe. Then, Annette – when we're all so sated that we can't do it again right now, no matter how much we want to ... Then, we'll go out. You and me and Pattie. We'll dress up fine and hit the town, and I'll buy my girls dinner in the best restaurant there is. And we'll be looking at each other all evening across the table, remembering what we've been doing; knowing that after we finish, we're going to go home and start all over again. Maybe you'll watch me and Pattie go at it to start with; hell, we could totally have a threesome. I think Pattie's got a strap-on somewhere, so maybe she can do you with that, while you suck my cock. How does that sound?'

It sounds pretty good to John. More than good. A dream – a fantasy come true. He drinks the last of his beer and looks ruefully at the two life-sized dolls opposite him, one blonde and busty, the other dark haired and petite.

'And maybe,' he says, 'some day, I'll get to say all this to a real woman ...'

Coming Home
by Dee Jaye

I was stunned the evening my new flatmate brought her boyfriend home. One lingering glance at the tall blond guy clutching Rachel's hand and the moistness that had tormented my pussy since early that morning welled up and started to seep into my knickers.

My own boyfriend should have been here lunch time. He'd been away for three months working on the oil rigs, and my hormones had been rioting at the thought of a good fuck with him. Especially since it was my 27th birthday, which meant he'd planned his timing to perfection. But when he'd phoned to say his plane had been delayed I could have screamed I felt so horny.

'Vicky, this is Pete,' my flatmate said. 'And that's his sister, Emily. She pointed to a petite younger girl standing the other side of him.'

'Hi.' I nodded twice, but didn't dare look into those piercing blue eyes again.

'Emily and I are going to work on that play I told you about,' she explained. 'Pete's come along to read the male part.'

'Great.' Rachel was into amateur dramatics. 'I'll get us a drink. What do you all fancy?'

As soon as the drinks were sorted I hurried off to my room where I kept my computer. I had to stay away from him. The chemistry was far too powerful, and it wouldn't be right to fuck my flatmate's boyfriend.

Except it was no refuge, for a short while later there was a tap on my door and I opened it to Rachel.

'Me and Emily are just popping out for a takeaway,' she said. 'Be about half an hour.'

The front door slammed. I squirmed on my swivel chair by the desk at the thought of being alone in the flat with Pete.

He must have thought the same, since a minute later he appeared in the doorway, a half smile on his lips, eyes heavy with lust.

Chemistry ruled. Foreplay was out of the question. I leapt out of the chair and made a grab for him, snatching kisses while he yanked off my knickers and I unzipped his jeans.

'We don't have long,' I gasped, freeing his cock and dropping to my knees.

'No,' he squealed, as my lips wrapped around the solid girth. 'Oh, yes,' he groaned, as I moved my head slowly backwards and forwards, then flicked the tip with my tongue until I could taste the bitter-sweetness of the leakage that preceded the flow.

'Stop, I'm coming,' he yelped. 'Quick, up here.' He reached under my armpits and almost threw me onto the bed.

Lifting my dress, I spread my legs wide and within moments felt his heavy, latex-clad prick plunge into my soaking hole.

'Yes, yes, fuck me, fuck me,' I squealed, in tune with the rhythm of his grunting. 'Come on, come on,' I urged, bucking my hips hard as I felt the approaching orgasm.

'Oh, fuck, fuck, fuck,' he gasped between gritted teeth, and as I felt his hot flood inside me I arched my back and shuddered with ecstasy as my own juices mingled with his come inside my throbbing cunt.

We couldn't have lain there recovering for more than two minutes when I heard the key in the lock.

'Shit,' I muttered, wincing with regret as his now semi-hard cock slid out of me and he leapt to his feet.

I'd just made it to the swivel chair and he was perched on the side of the bed with its pulled-together duvet when my door swung open.

'Problem solved,' I said to Rachel. 'I didn't realise your guy was so good with computers.'

Her dark eyebrows lifted quizzically. 'Neither did I.' She threw a glance round the room and I wished I'd opened the window. It must have been filled with the smell of sex. 'Come on, or the pizzas will be getting cold.'

'Right, I'll get some drinks.'

Fortunately I'd stocked up on a good variety of alcohol ready for when my Dave got home. After all, I never knew if he'd be on his own or be bringing some "special" guests. I didn't mind either way. We both enjoyed a good fuck with someone different occasionally, and the not-knowing always gave me an extra frisson of excitement.

We girls shared a bottle of wine. Well, to start with anyway, for one soon led to another. Meanwhile, Pete knocked back a few cans of lager and it was getting late by the time the three of them decided they ought to at least do a bit of work on the play before they got sozzled.

I left them to it, heading into the kitchen to clear up and do some sorting. It must have been an hour or so later when the door opened and closed, giving me a quick blast of rock music from the living-room. I swivelled round to see Pete smiling down at me.

'Hi,' he said, stepping closer.

'What are you doing?' I threw a glance past him. 'Rachel's in the next room.'

Smiling wickedly, he grabbed my shoulders and pulled me towards him.

'You're not listening,' I said, swallowing hard as I put my palms to his chest.

'Stop worrying,' he murmured in my ear. 'They've gone into Rachel's room to play some computer game.'

Then his lips met mine and I couldn't resist. Wet hands or not, I grabbed his tight little bum and ground my hips against the bulge inside his trousers.

His tongue carried on probing while he slid a hand down between our bodies and reached under my skirt. Then he stopped and pulled back his head so he could see my face.

'So, it's little Miss No-Knickers, is it?' he said, grinning as he shoved two finger into my welcoming slit.

'Fucking hell,' I whimpered, my knees buckling slightly when his fingers began to move slowly in and out. 'We shouldn't be doing this. If one of the others came in...' I stopped there, gasping as one of his fingers hit my g-spot.

And then the kitchen door did swing open.

We both froze as a dishevelled Emily yawned her way in. I turned half away from Pete and gurgled a plate into the sink full of tepid water.

But he didn't let up. I bit my bottom lip, trying not to react as he continued to finger-fuck me.

As it was, Pete's sister seemed hardly aware of us. She muttered something unintelligible, took a cold bottle of wine from the fridge, then drifted back out.

Suddenly I felt light-headed. My whole body was tingling, every nerve ending seemed to have its own unique sensation. Now my shaking legs gave way entirely, and Pete lowered me gently to the tiled floor, that finger still playing on my g-spot while his thumb massaged my clit making me writhe with pleasure.

'This is insane,' I panted. 'What if they come in again?'

'We'll be fine. They've got their drinks now.'

I wanted to believe him. Nothing else mattered. Tugging his wet fingers from inside me I transferred them to my mouth. As I sucked on them I unhooked his belt, yanked his trousers down, and raising my hips off the floor grabbed his sensitively covered rock-hard cock and plunged it into my drenched pussy.

'Hurry up,' I begged, digging my nails into his clenched buttocks. 'Or I'll beat you to it.'

'No way,' he grunted, pounding harder.

Seconds later we came together, both screeching our satisfaction between gritted teeth. And Pete had just rolled away when once more the kitchen door opened.

I sprang to my feet and grabbed a yellow duster I'd been using earlier. Pete frantically pulled up his trousers and pretended he'd just picked something off the floor. I could only hope that with the fridge where it was, and the subdued under-shelf lighting, his girlfriend might not have noticed.

Yeah, right.

Rachel's gaze switched between me and Pete.

'It's not as bad as you think,' I blustered. 'We only ...' My voice died as she scurried back out.

What had I done? I was at a loss. My head was spinning, my pulse played bongos while warm come flowed down the inside of my thighs. I wanted to run and hide, but was still rooted to the spot when Rachel reappeared with Emily in tow.

'I'm sorry, it was the drink,' I babbled. I turned to Pete. 'Tell her. Tell her it didn't mean anything – that it won't happen again.'

Then, to my surprise, Rachel grinned. 'There's nothing to tell,' she said. 'I didn't want to rock the boat, either.'

I frowned. The music outside stopped abruptly, leaving a tense silence.

Rachel broke it. 'The thing is, Vicky, you've done me a favour. You see, Pete's only here with us as a decoy. A decoy under oath, that is.'

'A decoy? An oath?' I threw a glance at Pete. He gave me a sheepish smile.

'Exactly. I made him promise not to say anything or he'd lose a best friend,' Rachel went on. 'The thing is, being a new lodger I was finding it difficult to tell you. But knowing you and Pete have got it together makes all the difference.'

With that, she reached out and took Emily's hand in hers.

I looked from her to the younger girl's blushing cheeks and the penny dropped. Shaking my head, I faced Pete. 'I suppose the next thing you're going to tell me is that Emily's not your sister.'

He smiled. 'Well, now we've got that out of the way it's time for Vicky's present. Right, girls?'

'Absolutely,' they chorused. 'Come on.'

'What? What are you doing?' I demanded, as the two girls grabbed my arms and led me into the living-room, now lit only by half a dozen flickering candles.

'We forgot your birthday card,' said Pete, tugging down the zip on my dress. 'So we thought we'd give you a present instead.'

'You don't have to do that,' I gasped, as my bra fell

away and I felt cool air on my achingly hard nipples.

'Wanna bet?' Rachel broke in. She was already as naked as I was, her ample tits swinging while she rested her hands on my shoulders and pushed me to the carpet.

Pete turned away. 'Won't be long,' he said, and headed off down the hallway presumably to the bathroom.

'Let's have you then.' This time the nude Emily with her petite, boyish figure encouraged me backwards until I was laid out flat.

She laid out, too, on top of me, her firm little tits squashed against mine, her size eight body no weight at all, her velvety lips dabbing at mine seeking a response.

It was a whole new experience for me, feeling a girl's smooth, delicate skin along my length and having her tongue flick at me impatiently. I succumbed, tasted her orange lipstick, then opened my mouth and basked in the way our tongues weaved and dived the french way, while down below I could feel my pussy becoming hotter and wetter by the second.

Too soon she stopped, and I sighed as her mouth left mine. Although it didn't leave my body. Instead, she snaked downwards, leaving a kiss on each of my jutting, hypersensitive nipples, the soft part of my belly, then over the mound to where my throbbing clit waited in anticipation.

Ah, luxury. That tongue I'd sucked only seconds ago was now doing the same thing to my erect clit.

Meanwhile Rachel had leaned over me, and while my hips squirmed with pleasure I nibbled and nipped at a pair of breasts that were far fuller than mine.

That didn't last long, either. My flatmate moved away, only this time upwards until she was on her knees with her crotch straddling my face. She was facing away from me, sitting up straight, and I could smell the unfamiliar but heady aroma of her vagina, see her labia spread wide. I watched, fascinated, as those luscious lower lips moved ever closer. At last they sank on to my face and I had a second new, breathtaking experience of shoving my tongue into the dark dampness of another girl's pussy.

I could see or hear almost nothing as I lapped the depths of Rachel's hole. But the very act must have heightened my senses, since now Emily's persistent licking and tugging at my clit was driving my juices forwards at a frantic rate. My hips started to buck helplessly, then I orgasmed with a loud moan into Rachel's fleshy, squirming crotch. At the other end I could feel my juices spurting out on to Emily and I opened my mouth to shout to the world how wonderful it was. But as I did so Rachel gushed her load, too, and after a sample of what tasted like burnt honey I gobbled up as much as I could.

'I ... I don't know what to say,' I began, when Emily's head left my thighs and Rachel shifted away from my face to kneel on the carpet beside me.

'There's no need,' said my flatmate. 'Just turn over, relax, and go with the flow.'

I did as she asked, turning over on to my front. But not before I had a glimpse of the bottom half of a naked male behind her, the sheath on his massive erection glistening in the candlelight with each step he took.

He disappeared from view. I looked left and right as best I could facing the floor, and saw both Rachel and Emily kneeling either side of me smiling wickedly. As I wondered what was going on, each of them slipped a hand beneath my hips.

'Here we go.'

They pushed upwards. My knees automatically moved forwards causing my bum to lift in the air and my back to form a hollow, given that my head remained resting on my arms.

'Brilliant. Don't move.'

I remained there, aware of how exposed I was. A moment later I winced as something smacked my bare bum, then two rough hands grabbed the tops of my thighs and spread them wide. I sighed as a man's cock slipped easily into my still sopping wet cunt and began to thrust in and out. It felt good. I needed no urging, but began to move backwards and forwards in time with his rhythm.

As I did so Rachel left my side and Emily changed her position. Soon she was lying on her back in front of me, bent legs either side of my head, inching towards me until her crotch was right up to my face. I knew exactly what she wanted, and I eagerly licked her clean-shaven pussy each time the cock inside my own hole thrust me forwards.

Then suddenly the thrusting halted and the hot cock withdrew.

'No,' I whimpered, waggling my rear. 'You can't stop now.'

'Patience,' I heard Rachel say. At least I thought it was her, although it did sound like her mouth was very full. 'It's only for a moment.'

Emily swung her leg over my head and her little pink pussy moved away. Instantly Pete took her place, feet towards me, his thick rigid dick pointing at the ceiling. He gestured, palm upwards, indicating that I should raise myself on to my hands. I did, and once in the doggy position he wriggled along the carpet below me. Onwards he came until his cock was beneath my mouth.

I bent my head and sucked the raspberry-tasting rubber, but only for a moment. He carried on down until his dick was pushing against my vulva.

'On you go,' he said hoarsely.

I didn't hesitate. Reaching back I found that steel-hard erection and pushed it into my welcoming slit. Then, sighing happily, I lowered myself onto it right up to the hilt.

'Better like this,' he murmured, grasping my shoulders and bending me forwards so we could kiss.

That's when it happened. That's when I felt another pair of hands spread the cheeks of my arse wide, and a finger bathed in something cool and squishy rubbed against my sensitive, virginal rosebud.

I jumped, lifted my lips from Pete's and stared at him in wonder. He grinned up at me. At the same time something much larger than a finger brushed against my anus.

'Oh,' I squeaked, my eyes wide as it found the opening and pushed slowly inwards.

I bit my lip as it entered, expecting it to hurt, but the lubrication must have done the trick. If there was any pain it was overwhelmed by the pleasure.

Emily was still beside me, her hand rubbing my back while Pete massaged her vagina with an outstretched hand.

I'd lost sight of Rachel a while ago and wondered what she was using back there to pleasure me. My girlfriends had talked about strap-ons and I'd seen them in shops, but I never thought the day would arrive when someone would be using one on me. Nor did I imagine that it would feel so real.

At last the steady penetration into my rear ceased and the withdrawal began.

Beneath me Pete must have realised. 'Right, then,' he murmured. Then I felt his cock begin to move smoothly in and out.

The shaft up my arse did the same, a hand occasionally smacking my cheeks as I revelled in yet another first time experience, having both my holes stuffed with two huge dicks at the same time.

None of us held out for long.

Pete shot his load first. 'Fucking he-e-ell!' he yelled, wrapping his arms around my shoulders and squeezing hard as his hot come spurted into me.

That gave me a boost. I could feel my orgasm gathering pace as the rod up my rear pulsed faster and faster.

But Emily beat me to it. 'Yes ... yes ... yes!' she shrieked, and glancing to my right I saw her fall backwards with Rachel on top of her.

With Rachel? I grimaced as I bucked and jerked with the excited ramming from behind. If my flatmate was there with Emily who was …?

Then it dawned on me. There'd been a time when Rachel had been sitting on my face and I could see or hear next to nothing. It was a set-up. The whole thing had been planned!

'Happy birthday, you lovely fucking little whore,' the man behind me yelled while he pumped his come into my bumhole.

'Dave, you big smart bastard,' I screamed as my juices flooded out on to Pete's dick and balls. 'You could have told me you were home already.'

Xcite

Xcite Books help make loving better with a wide range of erotic books, eBooks and dating sites.

www.xcitebooks.com
www.xcitebooks.co.uk

facebook

Sign-up to our Facebook page for special offers and free gifts!